Praise for the Novels of

THE MAIDENSTON

"Sweet, light and as com... ... peppermint tea, O'Rourke's latest will please her fans."
—*Publishers Weekly*

"O'Rourke entices readers with her well-crafted second novel."
—*Romantic Times*

THE MAN WHO LOVED JANE AUSTEN

"With charm and wit, Sally Smith O'Rourke weaves an enchanting, clever and often haunting tale of high romance, of hearts reaching out to one another across the ages, and of the timeless search for true love. To be read with an expectation of pleasure."
—Peter Pezzelli, author of *Francesca's Kitchen*

"O'Rourke alternates between the past and the present in this fascinating novel that pays tribute to Jane Austen's enduring ideals of romantic love."
—*Booklist*

"In *The Man Who Loved Jane Austen*, Sally Smith O'Rourke confirms what readers have always hoped for—that Mr. Darcy is real, and that he's even more dashing and romantic than we imagined. This wonderfully conceived novel is fresh, original and rewarding."
—Susan Wiggs

"For all those readers who longed for Jane Austen to have the kind of love she gave her characters—and for all those readers who longed to have Fitzwilliam Darcy to themselves. Sally Smith O'Rourke gives us access to one of our most beloved writers and our favorite characters. A wonderful, magical read."
—Jessica Barksdale Inclan

Books by Sally Smith O'Rourke

THE MAN WHO LOVED JANE AUSTEN

THE MAIDENSTONE LIGHTHOUSE

CHRISTMAS AT SEA PINES COTTAGE

Published by Kensington Publishing Corporation

CHRISTMAS AT
SEA PINES COTTAGE

SALLY SMITH O'ROURKE

KENSINGTON PUBLISHING CORP.
http://www.kensingtonbooks.com

KENSINGTON BOOKS are published by

Kensington Publishing Corp.
850 Third Avenue
New York, NY 10022

Copyright © 2008 by Michael O'Rourke and Sally Smith O'Rourke

All rights reserved. No part of this book may be reproduced in any form or by any means without the prior written consent of the Publisher, excepting brief quotes used in reviews.

All Kensington Titles, Imprints, and Distributed Lines are available at special quantity discounts for bulk purchases for sales promotions, premiums, fund-raising, and educational or institutional use.

Special book excerpts or customized printings can also be created to fit specific needs. For details, write or phone the office of the Kensington special sales manager: Kensington Publishing Corp., 850 Third Avenue, New York, NY 10022, attn: Special Sales Department, Phone: 1-800-221-2647.

Kensington and the K logo Reg. U.S. Pat & TM Off.

ISBN-13: 978-0-7582-3798-9
ISBN-10: 0-7582-3798-7

First Trade Paperback Printing: October 2008
First Mass Market Printing: December 2008

10 9 8 7 6 5 4 3 2 1

Printed in the United States of America

For Nicholas
with love from
Cubby and Da

And for Lily
who let us feel
an angel's touch and
see an angel's smile

Foreword

Michael O'Rourke and I spent almost three decades together as friends, partners, soul mates, as well as husband and wife. Our life together was the ultimate collaboration, and out of that and our love came many projects, including *The Man Who Loved Jane Austen*, *The Maidenstone Lighthouse* and *Christmas at Sea Pines Cottage*.

Christmas at Sea Pines Cottage is a very special story and holds a singular place in my heart. "Meteor's Tale," as it was originally titled, was created not only out of our love for each other but also for the love of our grandson, Nicholas.

Nicky wanted a "big" dog like a Golden Retriever, but his mom, Kelly, felt that since she would be doing the bulk of the care a smaller, more manageable pet would be better. So Nicky had to settle for a stuffed Golden Retriever and Jenna, a larger-sized Pomeranian. A very cute Pomeranian.

But out of Nicky's desire for a big dog came Meteor's Tale, the story of a loving family told through the eyes of the family's pet Golden Retriever. Only Mike would have thought of an idea like that, to tell a dog's story in the first person.

After he completed the original story, we discussed turning it into a Christmas story, an evergreen project, he called it. Unfortunately, we lost him before we were able to carry out the ideas we had to make it a holiday tale.

Mike's amazing talent and gifted writing were silenced in 2001. Unwilling to let his work die with him and, with the help of Kensington Publishing, Michael's genius will bring pleasure to many people for years to come.

As for *Christmas at Sea Pines Cottage,* I took the plans we made and turned "Meteor's Tale" into the holiday story we envisioned. So experience it. Make it a new tradition for you and your family to enjoy, year after year.

The merriest of Christmases to you and yours.

Affectionately,
Cubby and Da

Prologue

The big yellow school bus eased to a stop amid the squeal of air brakes. By the time the young boy jumped down from the bottommost step, the puppies were already at the gate jumping and yipping their collective greeting.

The child unlatched the gate, and, as he stepped through, was besieged by seven wiggly pups. He fell giggling to the ground as his face and neck were thoroughly licked and nuzzled.

The sound of his name brought him to his feet with the puppies scurrying around him, vying for a free hand to receive his pats.

An older boy stood outside the gate. "Mom wants you to go in and rest, or you won't be able to go trick-or-treating tonight."

The small boy ruffled the ears of each of the seven puppies and then left, skipping alongside his brother.

The older brother said with some disdain, "Just because Dad breeds dogs doesn't mean the puppies are yours."

Without responding, as young children are wont to do, he asked his big brother, "Are you taking me trick-or-treating or is Mom?"

Shaking his head at the unheeded warning he conceded, "I am. Mom thinks I'm too old; the only way she'd let me go was by my agreeing to take you. So Jimmy, Bobby and their pesky little brothers are coming over, and we're all going together."

The younger brother excitedly said, "Are you going to dress up, too?"

Grabbing his little brother up and pretending to carry him off, the older brother replied, "Yeah, I'm going to be a pirate. Argh."

The little boy giggled with pleasure and expectation.

⚜

Night fell, and the only sound was the wind rustling the trees that surrounded the kennels.

Snuggly warm in the embrace of his siblings, the young pup suddenly raised his head, his acute hearing discerning a sound other than the wind. He sniffed the air, his sensitive nose recognizing the older of the two boys who had visited them earlier in the day.

The puppy got up and trotted to the gate in anticipation of a treat or an ear rub. The other puppies followed, roused by his movement. They waited at the locked gate, sniffing the air and milling around it.

Suddenly, three human forms darted out of the darkness, causing the motion-controlled lights to come on. As they ran past the puppies' enclosure, one of them tossed something into the center of the yard.

Expecting some tasty treat, the puppies rushed to where the object lay. One pup nudged the thing with his nose, in spite of the strange hissing noise it made, and yelped when a small spark singed the fur of his muzzle. The other puppies stood back, away from the thing as it continued to hiss and spark.

The light at the end of it grew brighter as it started to spin in a circle. As the puppies drew farther away from it, the objectionable thing started exploding: one small explosion quickly followed another. The animals began running helter-skelter to get away from the horrid noise and find safety, as they piled into the deepest corner of the kennel. After what seemed an interminable time, the loud popping finally stopped.

The puppies' sensitive ears were still ringing when the three human boys unlocked the gate, rushed in and picked up the offending object.

The boy the pup recognized said, "Gotta get this out of here. My dad will kill me if he finds out about this."

Another boy said, as they locked the gate and walked away, "Yeah, but did you see the way they all scattered and whined?"

Chapter 1

METEOR

Meteor is my name.

That is, of course, my human name. Or, more precisely, since I am not a human myself, it is the name that was bestowed upon me by Robert on the day I first arrived here at the gray shingled cottage sheltered among the pines on the wild dunes of Cape Fear.

Though my keen hunter's eyes have since grown dim with the passage of too many autumns, each wondrous detail of the bright November afternoon when I was named remains as fresh and untarnished within my memory as if it had happened today.

It was the day after what humans call Thanksgiving. In the two weeks preceding, Sam had been able to sell my brothers and sisters "as pets." It disgusted him that we would never be of value as anything but household pets, and he was glad to be rid of us. I alone remained.

After a whispered conversation with his female counterpart, I was unceremoniously put in a cardboard box in the back of Sam's truck. But before

Sam could drive away, the woman returned and secured a red and green bow around my neck, saying I was now a Christmas puppy. Then she gave me some wonderful meat that she said was left over from dinner the day before.

"Be good," she whispered as she kissed my nose.

Jumping down from the flat bed of the truck, she walked around to the window and kissed Sam, gently reminding him that I was just a puppy. Sam snorted as the truck rumbled off past the sign identifying what had been my domicile, Prairiewood Kennels—Home of Champion Retrievers.

The truck came to a stop at a place with which I was unfamiliar. I could smell the sea and feel its mist on my fur. After peering over the edge of the truck I retreated again to the box, shivering from an unnamed fear rather than the fierce cold wind that was blowing in from the restless sea.

Robert, at twenty-four, was in the very prime of his youth then. Tall and tan and deep-chested, his tangled brown hair streaked gold from the white hot sun of the summer, he appeared like a young god to the bewildered pup he found shivering in the corner of a soggy corrugated box in the back of Sam Wilson's old pickup truck.

I was that frightened pup.

Sick and dizzy from the noxious exhaust fumes that had swirled about me throughout a long, cold ride in the clattering truck bed, my future at that moment could not have seemed more dismal. Sam Wilson had made it clear that I was a disgrace in his eyes, as well as those of any other human who knew and seriously bred dogs for hunting in the great marshlands that dominate this sparsely inhabited region of the North Carolina coast.

My life was over before it had properly begun. Or so I had believed then. Less than a span of seasons had passed since I had been weaned from my mother's milk. But though I was bright of eye and swift of foot, and despite my noble blood and the fine, strong features that had seemed to promise a happy lifetime filled with the honors that, rightly, accrue to champion retrievers, I had become an embarrassing burden to Sam Wilson, a useless creature to be disposed of as quickly and as quietly as possible.

Cowering in the corner of my foul box that afternoon, I was unwilling even to look up at the curious young man who had climbed onto the truck to look me over. Instead, I curled up in my box and whimpered at the cruel circumstance that had so abruptly reduced my life to such a sorry state. Then, without warning, I felt myself being hoisted high into the air, held up and closely scrutinized by Robert's calm gray eyes.

Oh, those eyes! Warm and compassionate and wise beyond the years reflected in the smooth, unlined face that held them, they bored into my very soul, searching there for something—I knew not what—but betraying no trace of the naked contempt I had so lately seen in the eyes of Sam Wilson when he looked at me.

Suddenly, my soul was filled with an unreasonable hope. Perhaps this human would give me another chance to prove my worth. Although truly I dreaded the prospect of returning to the scene of my humiliation and was not at all certain that I would not fail again, still, I forced myself to cease my whimpering. And as pups will often do when they sense true goodness and compassion radiating from a human being, I lavishly licked Robert's square, handsome face.

To my great surprise and joy, he laughed out loud, a soft baritone sound that made me shiver with such pleasure that I even forgot for the moment the terrors of the grim trial I had so recently failed. Then Robert set me on the sandy ground and tossed a bit of driftwood far down the beach. It disappeared among the curling green waves that were crashing onto the cold sands in advance of a waiting Arctic storm moving in from the east.

Gulping in a huge breath of clean sea air, I felt my sickness vanish as if by magic. And I ran after that twisted stick of wood as though my very life depended upon it, which, in a way, I was certain that it did. For, from the moment I heard Robert's exuberant laughter and looked into those placid gray eyes, I had decided that my only chance for happiness lay in gaining the approval of this young, handsome human.

Pounding into the chilly backwash of a receding wave, I pounced on the thrown driftwood with a spectacular splash. Then, gripping the trophy tightly in my jaws, I dashed back to where the men were standing and heard Sam Wilson talking in low, serious tones.

My heart sank as I trotted up all dripping from the salty water to drop the stick like an offering at Robert's booted feet.

Sam Wilson—who, for all his understandable lack of warmth toward me, was a fair and honest man—was carefully explaining to Robert in his slow Elizabethan accent typical of some native Outer Bankers that he wanted it clearly understood I would never be useful as a hunting dog.

"He will not stand to guns," Wilson proclaimed, casting a disgusted look my way. What he meant, of course, was that the sound of a hunter's rifle going off just above my head did remind me of that horrible night in the kennel.

For though Sam trained me to know that the dreaded explosion would come and not harm me and I could always steel myself to point the game and stand rock steady, ultimately the awful boom of the rifle shot never failed to take me by surprise, hurting my sensitive ears and throwing me into a blind panic from which my only instinct was to flee.

On that fateful November morning, after endless working sessions on home ground, Sam Wilson had taken me, along with my brothers and sisters, out of our kennel for what he called a test. A test of what, we had no idea, but leaving the pen that had become a constant reminder of our terror initially brought all of us joy. And we happily jumped into the bed of Sam's beat-up old pickup truck.

The trip was fairly short, although it was to a place none of us recognized. Sam allowed us to run free amid the tall trees with frosty fallen leaves crunching under our paws. After a short time of sniffing out a banquet of wildlife, we were all called back to the truck. Sam stood next to the battered old vehicle with a shotgun on his shoulder. The sight made my stomach start to churn.

Once we were all standing at point around him

amid the strange surroundings, Sam raised the gun and fired a single shot into the air, a shot that sent all of us fleeing like frightened squirrels into the sun-dappled autumn woods.

With his normally sallow cheeks as crimson as ripe apples, poor Sam had been forced to drag us all cowering from the woods, knowing that his months of breeding and training were a total loss, and not one of us would ever be a gun dog. His anger at the time, due to the energy and money lost, was palpable even to seven terrified pups. There would never be a champion hunter among us.

"I do not hunt," Robert quietly replied after Sam Wilson had said his piece. Then he bent and gently ran his fingers through the thick mat of wet fur just behind my neck. "Nor do I ever intend to hunt," he continued. "But I am going to be wintering over here on the cape this year." He jerked his chin toward the gray, shingled cottage half hidden among the blowing pines, "and I think that I'd enjoy having this little guy around to keep me company."

Sam Wilson nodded and cast a dour look at the pair of us, the dog that couldn't stand to guns and the strange young man who didn't hunt and, to boot, was planning on spending a harsh Cape Fear winter in an isolated cottage on this remote coastal island, far from others of his kind. "Suit yourself," he said in a tone that seemed to imply that Robert and I deserved each other.

Until that moment, I had believed that I completely understood Sam Wilson's motive for bringing me out to this desolate island and its strange inhabitant. It had seemed obvious that he was hoping to recoup some portion of the feed and vet bills he had lavished on what had turned out to be a useless hunting dog by selling me to a lonely man who wanted only companionship. Therefore I was puzzled when the handful of wrinkled bills that Robert offered him were gruffly refused.

"No sir," said Sam Wilson, sweeping his old felt hat from his pale, balding head and looking down uneasily at his feet. "I could not take money from a man who has given what you have given for your country. The whelp is yours, if you want him." And with that, he clapped the hat back onto his head, climbed into his old truck and wished Robert a Merry Christmas as he drove away.

"Well now, you're the first good thing I've ever gotten out of that damned war and a Christmas present to boot," Robert laughed as we watched Sam's pickup disappear behind a line of dunes. When it was gone, he looked down at me with a grin.

"Now, what shall I call you?" he asked and bent to retrieve the soggy stick of driftwood as he hurled it skyward once more. I joyously streaked down to the beach with the chilly November sunlight flashing like quicksilver against my glistening amber coat.

"Meteor!" I heard him call as I plunged headlong into the bone-chilling maw of a towering Atlantic comber. "Seeing you run like that reminds me of a meteor streaking into the sea."

Thus I got my human name. And thus began my life here at Sea Pines Cottage. It has been a life that I would not exchange for any other, even were the Maker in His wisdom to grant me an endless span of seasons in this world.

For mine has been a life that any dog would envy.

A life built on unconditional love.

Chapter 2

SEA PINES COTTAGE

With the pale sun slipping behind the dunes and a bank of dirty storm clouds sliding ominously across the slate-gray sea, I trotted up a sandy path at Robert's heels on that November afternoon long ago. If I noticed then the odd stiffness in his gait or the one knee that seemed not to bend at all as he walked, I do not remember it. But then I was little more than a foolish pup at the time, and a very excited one at that.

At the top of the path we stepped into the shadows of a miniature pine forest sheltered among the dunes and onto a soft brown carpet of fallen needles. Robert stopped there to lean heavily against the trunk of a tree.

"Well, Meteor," he said, "what do you think of the place?"

Raising my nose from its delightful exploration of the fragrant forest floor, which was rich with the tantalizing scents of field mice and hare, and more varieties of seabirds than I could name, I looked up to see my handsome young master gazing fondly at the weathered old cottage nestled in among the trees. Beneath a steeply peaked slate roof thickly blanketed in pine needles, the walls of the little structure were sheathed in rough gray shingles of many sizes that reached right down to the ground.

Identical mullioned windows containing sparkling panes of wavy antique glass were precisely situated on either side of the scarred oak door, an attempt on the part of the original builder, I think, to impart some sense of balance to the ramshackle fisherman's dwelling. However, the placement of those two small windows at an equal distance from the cottage door only accentuated the wandering uneven lines of the hand-cut shingles. And I had the unsettling impression that the whole cottage was leaning drunkenly seaward and might tumble over onto its side at any moment.

Still, happy just to be away from Sam Wilson, I yipped cheerfully and rushed ahead to politely sniff the low front stoop. Grinning with pleasure at my seeming excitement, Robert hurried up the path and opened the rounded oak door for me. I hesitated on the threshold, for I had never been allowed inside a proper human house before, since I had lived a kennel existence up to then. But with Robert's encouraging smile prompting me to enter, I stepped inside and gazed about in wonder at the dimly lit interior of my new home.

What can I say about Sea Pines Cottage that will not sound like the mere nostalgic ramblings of a rheumy old canine? How does one describe comfort and snugness and elemental feelings of well-being that reach out welcoming arms to surround and embrace one's very soul? Sea Pines Cottage possessed those qualities, and more, exuding an indefinable impression that one could rest safe within its walls, protected there from all harm.

Unlike the dun exterior of the cottage, with its colorless shingled walls and sagging slate roof, the big main room on the ground floor fairly glowed with the richness of lovingly varnished woods and warm fabrics. Beneath the heavy ceiling beams, soft rugs woven from cleverly twisted strands of gaily colored rags dotted the polished floorboards like so many flowercovered islands. The softly cushioned wooden furniture was draped with bright woolen throws and intricately patterned Indian blankets, a few of which also hung on the pine-paneled walls beside groups of faded photos and one truly gigantic sailfish trophy.

But perhaps the very best feature of the room was the big stone fireplace at its far end. Broad and smoke-blackened with age beneath a heavy wooden mantle sawed from the cracked timbers of a sailing ship that had perished long ago on the rocks of Cape Fear, the fireplace had been built to serve as the main room's primary source of both heat and light.

As if to confirm its homely utilitarian purpose, a driftwood fire was crackling in the fireplace beneath a bubbling kettle hung on a stout iron hook that could be swung out over the hearth. And from the fire-stained vessel, there issued the delightful smell of a hearty stew that was almost ready to be eaten.

In a far corner of the room, beneath many

shelves of well-worn books, sat the wide table where Robert did his work. The table contained only a pressure lantern—for, back then, the cottage had no electricity or any other modern conveniences—stacks of paper and a tall, old-fashioned typewriting machine.

As it was on that first day, the main room of Sea Pines Cottage remains fixed in my mind's eye as the most wonderful room that I have ever seen.

Robert led me to the hearth and bade me sit by the fire. I gladly complied, for I was thoroughly chilled from my recent immersions in the sea, and my coat was still damp. As I sat there soaking in the delicious warmth radiating from the flat stones, Robert vanished through a low doorway that I later learned led to the kitchen, a modest affair containing cabinets, an old wood stove and a hand-operated pump.

He returned a moment later, carrying a rough strip of toweling and a flat tin pan. My mouth watered uncontrollably as I watched him swing the heavy cauldron out over the hearth and transfer several chunks of steaming beef onto the pan. These he covered with ladles full of dark, rich gravy. Then, putting the pan aside to cool, he set about roughly drying my coat, toweling and rubbing the yellow fur until I fairly glowed all over.

When he had finished drying me, Robert carried the pan to a nook by the hinged woodbox at the end of the hearth and placed it there.

"This will be your corner," he told me with quiet authority. "When I need peace and quiet to do my work, this is where you must stay." He made a small gesture with his hand, indicating that I might attack the wondrous meal he had set for me, which I did with such puppyish enthusiasm that, afterwards, I confess, I had to be toweled dry all over again, in order to remove all of the gravy that had splashed onto me.

Daylight was quickly fading, and the first strong gusts of the oncoming Arctic storm were bending the tops of the pines as Robert led me outside once more. Circling around behind the cottage, he stepped into a large shed containing the canvas-shrouded form of a little sailing sloop. Selecting a big ring of keys and a lantern from a peg, he led me down another long path between the dunes and out onto the cold, windswept beach.

The angry green waves were advancing onto the sands with growing fury as we walked toward the imposing white tower of a brick lighthouse set high atop a jumble of massive granite boulders half a mile away at the tip end of the cape. Squinting against the sting of the blowing sand and salt spray that filled the air, we passed a tumble-down lightkeeper's house with its empty windows rattling in the gale.

The house, Robert explained over the roar of wind and sea, was a relic from the days before satellites and radios, when keeping the lighthouses beaming out their lifesaving signals to ships in these stormy and treacherous waters was a vital and honored profession requiring the full attention of a lightkeeper and his whole family.

Nowadays, he added with a trace of sadness in his voice for something that had been lost and could never be regained, most of the coastal lights were automated affairs requiring only the occasional attention of part-time lightkeepers like himself, men chosen for no other reasons than that they lived nearby and could be counted upon to monitor daily the diesel generators that powered the beacons and confirm the functioning of the lights themselves.

Jangling the big ring of keys against the locked steel door at the base of the round brick tower, Robert let us into the lighthouse, which was filled with throbbing noise and the stink of diesel fuel. After carefully checking the generator tanks and making a note on a chart attached to a clipboard on the wall, he craned his neck and peered up the rusting metal stairs that spiraled away into the top of the tall structure. "Well, come along," he said, climbing wearily onto the first step. "We have to check the beacon now."

Step by painful step, Robert climbed to the top of those endless winding steps without stopping. When we finally reached the cramped space on top, where the huge lenses of the dazzling beacon swiveled silently behind their protective greenhouse of rain-splattered glass, he sank onto a small stool, his handsome features drained of color.

After a few moments, he smiled and lifted me up to see the startling vista beyond the windows to seaward. As far as the eye could see, the ocean was a black, featureless desert topped by wind-whipped peaks of foam that were being shredded into long white streamers by the shrieking gale.

Trembling at the magnificent fury of the wild sea below, I was then let down to wait beneath Robert's stool as he circled the narrow catwalk around the whirling light, squirting dabs of oil onto the bronze bearings and measuring the rotations of the powerful beacon against a stopwatch.

When he was finished, he jotted some notes on another clipboard and laughed that rich, deep laugh that already touched my heart. "Everything is working perfectly, as usual," he sighed. "She turns exactly 360 degrees every minute and fifteen seconds, and all the gears and bearings are running smoothly and quietly. It never changes. I guess we could have saved ourselves that long climb tonight, Meteor."

I looked up at him and suddenly realized that my heart was beginning to pound. Something in his bantering tone, as Robert spoke about the light—a nugget of truth emerging from the actual words that he had spoken—said that no matter what the cost to himself in terms of pain or discomfort, this human would unfailingly make the steep and arduous climb up the winding stairs to the lighthouse tower each and every night simply because that was his duty.

As a canine and a thoroughbred of champion blood, I had been taught from birth to respect devotion to duty above all else. And Robert's unspoken message told me that I had not been mistaken, for he was a good and decent man deserving of all the love and loyalty I could give him.

With his duty done for another night, we descended from the tower and made our way back in the chilly air to the welcoming warmth of Sea Pines Cottage. I gratefully retreated to "my corner" by the woodbox as Robert prepared himself a plate of stew along with a mug of coffee and lit the bright pressure lantern on his work table.

While he ate his meal, he sat leafing through sheets of paper from a thin stack beside his writing machine. Presently, he set aside his plate and rolled a fresh sheet of paper into the typewriter and began to strike the keys with a loud, monotonous clacking sound that reverberated through the whole cottage.

Though my belly was full and my backside was pleasantly warm from the fire, I soon grew restless in my corner. I endured the onerous clacking for some minutes before deciding that it was time to play. Scooting across the room with my nails beating a loud tattoo on the polished floorboards, I slid to a clumsy halt at Robert's feet and leaped playfully into his lap, upsetting the mug of coffee in the process.

I found myself being lifted unceremoniously by the scruff of the neck and firmly deposited back in my corner. Robert's gray eyes flashed as he pointed to the dripping work table. "That table is strictly off-limits," he warned. "And, unless you favor spending all your evenings out in the cold shed, you will not disturb me again when I am working. Understood?"

I did not, of course, understand all of his words precisely. I don't believe that any canine is ever capable of translating the many confusing nuances of human speech into direct thoughts. But, just as his tone in the lighthouse had confirmed for me the true nature of Robert's noble character, his meaning about the table and his work could not have been more clear: in exchange for being allowed to share his wonderful house and his life, I must somehow learn to endure the long, boring periods when he was clacking away on his machine and would have no time for me.

So I placed my head upon my paws and attempted to look suitably remorseful as I lay by the fire, silently watching and dozing for many long hours as Robert returned to his table and focused his entire attention on the dreadful machine.

Even now, after a lifetime of human companionship, I am hard-pressed to understand fully mankind's fascination with those little marks that they so carefully impress on sheets of paper.

Oh, I understand well enough that it is a way they have devised of recording their thoughts and stories for other humans to see and study. And I will not deny that it is an admirable accomplishment and one no other earthly creatures have yet mastered. But what I cannot comprehend is how humans can bring themselves to shut out the truly wondrous marvels of the world that cry out for attention all about them, in order to stare for hours on end at those lifeless scratchings. How could a man like Robert ignore the entrancing blaze of a good crackling fire or the howling of the wind in the trees or the mysterious rustling of tiny feet in the rafters that simply demanded investigation?

It is beyond me to explain such behavior; for, to my simple dog's mind, the sights and sounds and smells of the real world would always hold sway over mere lines and lines of words on paper.

Perhaps it is not a thing that dogs were meant to understand. But I cannot help but feel that human lives are all the poorer for it.

After an interminable period of clacking on that first night, Robert finally stood up and extinguished the bright lantern. Then he stretched and took me to the door for a quick dash out into the cold rain.

When I returned from my business, all wet and shivering, he dried my coat again, then he lit a candle and led the way up a narrow wooden staircase to the top floor of the cottage. There, below the naked rafters of the steeply sloping roof, I discovered what I now believe was my favorite feature of Sea Pines Cottage, as it was then.

At the foot of a massive iron bed covered with a colorful down quilt, a large bay window afforded a breathtaking view of the wild, storm-tossed seascape through a gap in the sheltering dunes. Every minute and fifteen seconds the beacon of the Cape Fear lighthouse swept the horizon in a full circle, lighting the interior of the upstairs room bright as day for the briefest of instants as it passed.

Robert saw me staring out at the mesmerizing spectacle of nature untamed, and he smiled. "Like that view, do you?" he asked. When my gaze did not waver, he rummaged in an old trunk and produced a faded green blanket, which he folded onto the window seat for me. "Then that will be your special sleeping place," he declared.

He lifted me onto the blanket and laughed when I turned away from the spectacle beyond the window to gratefully lick his hand.

Settling down onto the wonderfully scratchy old blanket that was to be mine alone, I reflected on what a wonderful day it had turned out to be. Once more I was filled with the certain belief that I stood on the brink of a happy life, perhaps far happier than the one for which I had been trained and prepared for so long.

Then Robert unbuttoned his shirt and sat on the edge of his bed. And by the flickering candlelight he began to undress. All joy fled from my heart as I stared in horror at the cruel mechanical extension he removed from the stump of his missing leg. I started in fright as the ugly thing clumped heavily to the floor, a dead weight of metal and hideous pink plastic possessing no life of its own. Robert must have heard my gasp, for he turned to regard me. Then his eyes dropped to the stump of tortured flesh he wore.

"Sorry, I know it's not a very pretty thing," he apologized, misinterpreting the fear and pity he read in my eyes for a revulsion that I did not feel.

"This is something that men do to other men in wars," he explained in a voice that seemed suddenly small and far away. Then he extinguished the candle and fell back onto his pillows with a sigh.

"While I was being medi-vaced out the day it happened, I was all doped up with morphine. But I remember hearing somebody on the chopper say the Bad Guys got another one," he whispered in the darkness.

"I thought that was kind of a funny thing for them to say, like I was an unlucky actor in a cowboy movie," he said. "Don't you think that was a funny thing for them to say, Meteor?"

I made a small whimpering sound, hoping to ease the deep-seated anguish that I felt emanating in waves from the bed across the room. Then I lay there for a long time, counting the intervals of light and darkness as the great lighthouse beacon traveled through its tireless circle and trying to imagine how good it would feel to get my teeth into the evil Bad Guys who had done that terrible thing to Robert.

I did not sleep that night but remained alert on my warm blanket, listening closely to the rush of wind and rain through the swaying trees and the distant booming of the waves on the beach. For I was determined that, for as long as I lived, no Bad Guys would ever enter Sea Pines Cottage to make war on Robert again.

Chapter 3

A SPAN OF SEASONS

Autumn turned to winter, with the fierce Arctic gales sliding down from the far north one after another to vent their icy fury on the rugged beaches of Cape Fear.

No matter how foul the weather, Robert and I made our way out to the lighthouse at the end of the cape every day to check the generators and climb the steep winding stairs to the beacon above.

And when that duty was done, I dozed in my corner each night while Robert labored over his typewriting machine and later kept watch over him as he tossed and turned in his lonely bed. Sometimes he cried out in the night, shouting urgent warnings to comrades named Vic and Sarge and Billy. But, more often, he just moaned softly in his sleep, then rolled over and was silent again.

As difficult as those long winter nights were for me to endure, all of my days with Robert were filled with wondrous activities and accomplishments. For there was always driftwood to be gathered on the beach and dried behind the cottage, shingles to be split and replaced after each storm, and a hundred other things that constantly had to be tended and mended, in order to keep our cottage warm and snug under the ferocious assaults of wind and rain and cold.

As a change from those challenging everyday activities, we would sometimes climb into the old green Jeep that Robert kept covered with a heavy tarp behind the shed. Then, with me sitting proudly on the seat beside him, we would make the long and bumpy drive across the dunes to the narrow paved road that led across a low stone causeway to the little seaside hamlet of Thunderbolt.

There, Robert would take his carefully packaged sheets of paper into the tiny Thunderbolt Post Office to be sent away, and he would collect the slim white and tan envelopes containing papers that other humans had sent to him from far off places. Next, we would go to the dark and musty general store to buy all of the things we needed to maintain our lives at the cottage, and the curious eyes of the other humans would follow us as we moved along the aisles of canned goods and shovels and coiled rope.

When at last our purchases were all piled in the back of the Jeep and we were ready to return home, we always would stop at a little roadside stand for the delicious burgers that a jolly fat man cooked for us on a sizzling black grill.

How can I express the happiness and pride I felt on those trips to Thunderbolt? As a useful and respected companion, it was I who guarded the Jeep while Robert went off on his other errands.

As my reward I was always given my own juicy burger, served on a soft bun with plenty of ketchup and a thick slice of yellow cheese, but without the green leafy stuff that Robert had added to his. My mouth still waters at the memory of those burgers, although I cannot now recall the last time that I had one.

Robert didn't seem to enjoy our trips to Thunderbolt nearly as much as I. Because, except for the few words needed to make our purchases, seldom did he speak with the other humans he encountered in the town, though it often seemed clear to me that many of them, especially the young unmarried women, wished to speak with him.

Robert always changed in their presence, though, as his easy smile vanished behind a grim expression, like the sun slipping behind a bank of dark Atlantic storm clouds. And the jovial banter that I had come to expect from him on a daily basis was reduced to a few muttered phrases when he spoke to others of his kind. It was my impression in those days that Robert somehow feared other humans, rather than actually disliked them. But whatever emotions he was feeling about his fellow men then, the end result was the same: Robert had no friends or companions.

And he had no woman.

I think I was the only living creature to whom he revealed his true voice, and this he did frequently when we were alone, explaining to me everything he knew of nature and the sea, the workings of machines and a hundred other things. And, sometimes, on long winter nights when a big norther was blowing up around the snug co-

coon of our little cottage, Robert would read the stories to me that he wrote on his clacking typing machine. Many of the stories were beautiful tales of his life on the cape, surrounded by the constantly unfolding miracle of the wild creatures that lived in the pine forest, the changing of the seasons and the whimsical moods of the majestic, unpredictable sea.

The story that stayed longest in my memory was the tragic tale of his three friends, Vic and Sarge and Billy, all of whom had been lost on the same terrible day in the war, the day that the Bad Guys took Robert's leg away.

I did not like that story at all, for it left me feeling very sad and angry for many days afterwards.

By slow degrees, winter turned to spring. The fierce Arctic storms became fewer and were gradually reduced to chilly, infrequent squalls. Certain colorful birds that had not been seen on Cape Fear for many months returned to screech and chatter as they built their nests and found their mates among the pines of the miniature forest. Gradually, the blustery spring storms became the gentle rains of summer.

As the weather grew milder, Robert and I spent more and more of our time outdoors, as he painted and repaired the damage the harsh winter had wrought on the cottage.

One fine day when the blue sky was dotted with puffy little clusters of white clouds and a warm offshore breeze riffled the tops of the pines, Robert opened the shed behind the cottage and uncovered the little sailboat that he kept there.

Oh, it was a beautiful thing—that sleek little boat. It had a white wooden hull with darkly varnished trim and a tall mast that had to be set upright and then fastened in place with wire stays. On a cart with fat rubber tires, we hauled the boat down the steep path to the water's edge where we stepped her mast and hoisted her snowy sails. Then, as I stood nervously in the bow, barking out useless advice, Robert pushed the boat off into the swell of an incoming wave, and we were afloat with another great wave nearly towering over us.

I yipped in terror as a fresh gust of wind suddenly snapped the billowing sails taut as drumheads. And before the next rising wave could descend to crush our frail craft, Robert had jumped into the stern, and we had somehow turned and were skimming out to sea with a fine salt spray blowing back into our faces and the wire stays singing in the wind.

We sailed out to the smooth waters beyond the cape and cruised along the treacherous, beautiful North Carolina coast all that afternoon, and I cannot say that I had ever enjoyed a more glorious day.

After that, scarcely a day of fine summer weather passed that Robert and I did not sail the little sloop. Often, when we were safely offshore, away from the lines of breaking waves, he would let the sails down. Then, as we drifted on the backs of glassy swells with screeching gulls wheeling above our heads, Robert would fish with a hand line for our supper. On those occasions, he seldom failed to pull in a shining red snapper or a fat grouper, or another of the countless varieties of bottom feeders that grazed among the deadly rocks just beneath the surface.

Invariably, the day's catch would end up sizzling over an open fire on the beach that evening, the fresh, tender fillets sputtering on wooden skewers, while Robert drank cold beer from frosted cans and we watched the silent meteors plummeting into the sea or pondered the mysteries of the starry universe spread across the velvet sky above.

Through all of those wonderful days I continued to grow and mature, until I had reached full size and my golden coat had taken on the silky luster that in purebred retrievers comes only with adulthood. By that time also, I had been thoroughly trained in the special ways of my good master.

I believe I was as happy then as I had ever been in my life, but my happiness could not be called complete. For most nights, Robert continued to suffer from his restless tortured dreams of the war. Though I did my best to be as good and faithful a dog as any master ever had, Robert still had no other human being with whom he could truly share his innermost thoughts or the product of his fevered writings. And he had no one to comfort him in those long and lonely hours of the night.

Chapter 4

STORM

Almost before it had begun, it seemed the magical summer was coming to an end. The lingering traces of the wonderful season vanished one day in late August when we awoke to discover that a hurricane was racing with a vengeance toward Cape Fear.

All that morning Robert had huddled anxiously over the little portable radio that was our one reliable connection to the outside world. Listening to the ominous marine weather reports through bursts of crackling static, he drank endless cups of coffee and kept stepping outside to squint worriedly at the darkening sky.

The storm, according to the radio, had already wrought untold havoc in the West Indies, killing hundreds and leaving thousands more homeless. Now it had turned toward our exposed coastal island and was churning northward, preceded by deadly squalls that were filled with blinding rain and high winds. The lines of crashing surf had been rising higher and higher on our beach since well before dawn, and a record high tide was predicted for later in the day.

"We'll have to move the boat back up into her shed right away," Robert told me at the conclusion of the latest weather report, "or else we'll lose her to the tidal surge."

Robert's decision to return the sailboat to the protection of the shed behind the cottage underscored for me the seriousness with which he regarded the threat posed to us by the oncoming storm. For, while the little craft had rolled easily on her cart down the long steep path to the beach months before, getting her back up between the dunes quickly would be another matter altogether: one that would require an enormous amount of work, even with the aid of the powerful winch bolted to the front of the Jeep.

Once the little boat had been laid up in the shed behind the cottage, I knew she would not be brought out again that year. And so our idyllic summer would pass into memory.

During the fine weather that had prevailed all summer, we had kept the sloop pulled onto the sand above the high tide mark, protected by a flimsy canvas lean-to that left only her mast exposed. Another line squall was approaching as we hurried down the path between the dunes and stripped off the canvas cover preparatory to unstepping the mast and loading the sailboat onto her wheeled cart. The waves were advancing faster than Robert had calculated, and a frighteningly short distance away mighty green combers taller than Robert himself were rearing their frothy heads to hurl countless tons of water ever nearer to our frail craft.

With the canvas lean-to down, Robert climbed inside the hull and ducked into the sloop's little forward cabin in search of the tools with which to unfasten the taut wire stays that held the mast in place. I leaped up onto the foredeck and turned to regard the progress of the monster waves, which were crashing uncomfortably closer to our exposed position with each advancing set.

Then a monstrous breaker—taller than any I had seen so far—collapsed onto the shore with a thunderous roar, sending a foot of boiling froth to lick at the stern of the little boat before retreating back to sea. While I was barking furiously at the receding wave, I ran back to the cockpit and braced my front paws on the transom beside the tiller, prepared to warn Robert if another such giant should threaten.

That was when I saw the small dark object bobbing in the foam far out among the lines of approaching waves.

I ceased my frantic barking and narrowed my hunter's eyes, attempting to determine what the thing was. Though I had spied countless pieces of flotsam being swept in from the sea on other stormy days, this strange object was no piece of driftwood. Nor was it a resting seabird or a stray fisherman's float, or any of the dozens of other things I was used to seeing on the water. Round and dark and glistening, the subject of my scrutiny rolled in perfect rhythm with the motion of the swells, as if weighted from below by an unseen pendulum.

Another towering breaker rose up to disrupt my view of the thing. When that wave had crashed beneath the stern of the boat, soaking my fur with spray and nudging the hull ever so slightly, I saw that the floating object was closer than it had been before. Then it half-turned toward the beach, and I glimpsed a small, pale face and the orange collar of a flotation vest rising scant inches above the roiling waters.

I realized that I was looking at a human being adrift in the deadly surf!

I set up such a furious yapping that I must have telegraphed to Robert the helpless sense of terror I felt at the sight of that pathetic dot of humanity caught up in the raging sea. Before I could turn to summon him to see what I had found, Robert was at my side, staring in horror at the doomed castaway. Seconds dragged by like hours as we lost sight of the bobbing head behind another towering wave. When again we finally spotted it, we saw that it had moved no closer to our beach. Instead, caught in the strong riptide that paralleled the beach, it was rapidly being swept toward the jagged black rocks that jutted into the sea from the base of the lighthouse half a mile away.

Before I could fully comprehend what he was doing, Robert was racing to the bow of the boat and lifting a large coil of light manila hemp from the anchor locker.

For one heart-stopping moment I believed he was going to launch us into that deadly surf, a foolhardy move that was certain to bring about our instant destruction; for no vessel could possibly survive such sea conditions.

But Robert had something else in mind, something even more dangerous than launching the sloop. Opening his pocket knife, he slashed at the manila anchor line—the longest that we had on board. With the freed anchor line in his hand, he ran back to where I stood and quickly made it fast to the orange, horseshoe-shaped rescue float on the stern.

Next, Robert pulled on a life vest. With the heavy rescue float on one shoulder and the coil of anchor line on the other, he dropped to the sand and ran hobbling down the beach faster than I would have believed possible for a man with only one leg.

Another great wave smashed down just below the stern, and the hull of our boat lurched sideways in the race of foamy water that shot up onto the sand. I raised my voice, frantically attempting to warn Robert that our little craft would surely be swept away if something was not done immediately to save her. But Robert was by then a misty figure far down the beach, and my futile warning was carried away in the roar of wind and sea.

Halfway to the lighthouse, there stood a great concrete bollard with a rusting metal ring set in its top half-buried in the sand: a relic from the days when passing ships sent supplies and mail to the isolated lightkeeper in small boats that were hauled through the surf by ropes. I caught up with Robert there and found him looping the end of the manila line though the metal ring.

Looking out to sea, I suddenly understood what he meant to do: he had run ahead of the human who was being swept along toward the deadly rocks at the end of the cape, and now he was limping into the surf himself, reaching up to activate the flashing strobe light on the rescue float.

I flopped down onto my belly and whimpered at the sheer madness of Robert's plan. For it seemed obvious, even to a young dog, that if he somehow managed to get out beyond the line of breaking waves without being drowned or crushed to death, the chances that he could reach the castaway were pitifully small. And if by some miracle Robert did snag that poor unfortunate person before he was swept onto the rocks by the deadly riptide, the odds that the light manila line would hold or that Robert would have the strength to haul them both out of the cold, powerful current were even more infinitesimal.

I raised my head and howled a forlorn protest as Robert disappeared into the sheer, glassy face of an approaching breaker.

The manila line went as taut as one of the wire stays on the mast of our boat as I held my breath, waiting for him to reappear. Seconds dragged by—far too many seconds—with no sign of my beloved master. I felt the rapid thudding of my breaking heart and wondered what my life would be like without my dear Robert.

Then, far out among the waves, the flashing strobe on the rescue buoy flared above the swirling foam, and I saw that Robert was still hanging on. Much farther out, the other human was being rapidly propelled toward him, but it seemed certain that Robert could not get out that far before the other was swept past his position.

Three more times I endured the agony of seeing Robert disappear beneath the lines of incoming waves. And each time, when he finally reappeared, both he and the castaway seemed nearer to certain doom. I danced helplessly about on the damp, cold sand, and barked feeble encouragement until my throat was raw.

Then Robert vanished beneath the waves one final time.

An agonizing eternity passed until he reappeared, floating in the boiling trough between two huge swells. When the strobe light on the rescue buoy flared again, I saw that only a few feet separated Robert from the other human. Then, suddenly, he had the castaway in his arms and was struggling to pull them both back to shore.

Many minutes later, a huge green wave crashed onto the beach, depositing Robert and his bit of human salvage at my feet. He lay there gasping like a beached dolphin, and his lips were blue from the life-sapping cold. Beside him, unmoving in the flat, sunless daylight, lay the sodden form of the pitiful human that he had risked his life to rescue.

Chapter 5

OUR CASTAWAY

I remember little of how we managed to find our way back to the cottage in that storm. The wind was shrieking about us as the squall hit the shore with all its fury, whipping up clouds of sand and debris and driving horizontal sheets of cold, pelting rain directly into our burning eyes. With me at his side, Robert staggered up the beach carrying the limp form in his arms. Then, at some point, the sky turned as black as night, and I heard him shouting to me to go ahead and find the narrow path that would lead us up to the safety of the high dunes.

Wet and shivering and barely able to see, I think I may have glimpsed the shape of our pretty little sloop tumbling past us in the nightmare surf as I stopped to raise my sensitive nose into the howling storm. I thought I detected the faintest hint of wood smoke from the small fire we had left burning in the cottage, and I turned blindly in the direction from which I believed it came. I stumbled forward and gradually felt the ground beginning to rise beneath my feet.

Somehow, we managed to climb that steep path. At its top, the dark bulk of the cottage appeared as no more than a shape among the tortured swaying pines. Then, the scarred oak door was suddenly before us. The warm light of our refuge shone through the rain-streaked glass of the ornate little windows on either side of it. We pushed our way into the cottage and slammed the heavy door shut against the wind. At long last I felt the blessed warmth of heat radiating from the hearth stones of our massive fireplace on my salt-stung face.

Though his teeth were chattering and he could barely stand in the aftermath of the superhuman effort he had just expended, Robert focused his attention entirely on the human he had pulled from the sea. By the dim light of the guttering fire, I saw that the still form was dressed in denim trousers and a dark sailor's jacket. Robert gently laid the motionless body on the sofa before the fireplace. Pausing only long enough to throw a couple of thick driftwood logs onto the fire, he peeled off his dripping life vest and knelt beside the human.

The gusting wind whistled down the chimney, and the dry logs blazed up, as they filled the room with an orange glow that flickered and cast eerie dancing shadows on the walls.

In that strange glow, I saw Robert staring down into the chalky features of a young woman about his own age. Tawny golden hair clung wetly to her smooth forehead and curled down about her high, perfect cheekbones, and the corners of her full, bow-shaped lips hinted at a smile, as though she had moments before fallen asleep thinking of something pleasant.

"She's alive," Robert whispered, holding a trembling finger to the side of her pale throat. "But just barely." He lifted one of her eyelids to reveal an unseeing pupil of a startling sea-green hue. "Advanced hypothermia," he muttered darkly. "No telling how long she was in the water. We must get her warm."

And with that, he swiftly and efficiently began to undress the unconscious woman, lifting her like a baby to peel off the wet woolen sailor's coat and the loose-fitting T-shirt she wore underneath. Averting his eyes from her small naked breasts, he laid her back on the sofa. Then he took the soaked canvas shoes from her feet and, with some difficulty, removed the tight denim trousers that she wore, exposing her long slim legs to the red firelight.

Before I could wonder why he did not also remove the tiny silken underpants that remained clinging wetly to her narrow hips, Robert had tightly wrapped her in layer after layer of warm blankets and then jumped up to hurry out to the kitchen.

I heard the hand pump working on the wood countertop, and a moment later he returned with a dented kettle, which he placed on the iron hook over the fire to boil.

"First, we'll try to get some hot tea into you, then we've got to get you to a hospital," Robert softly whispered, gazing at the woman's placid features.

He suddenly turned and looked directly into my eyes for the first time since we had set out to move the sailboat an eternity before. "The causeway to the mainland will be three feet underwater by now, Meteor," he said with desperation in his voice. "I can think of only one other way in which we might possibly get some help out here."

Robert abruptly got to his feet and threw another log on the already blazing fire. Then he cocked his ear to the rattling of the wind-assailed slates on the cottage roof and looked up at the ceiling. "We'll wait for a bit and see whether this wind is going to die down before the main storm gets here," he said without lowering his gray eyes.

While we waited for the water to boil and the wind to abate, Robert went upstairs and changed out of his own wet clothes. I heard him softly cursing over the soaked straps and fittings of his artificial leg. Then the ugly thing clumped heavily to the floor, and he rummaged about in a closet. When he came down the stairs a few minutes later, he was wearing dry jeans and a heavy fisherman's sweater.

The clumsy artificial leg was gone. In its place, a shining rod of silvery metal with a rubber tip on its base protruded from the cuff of Robert's trousers.

He saw me looking at the metal rod and shook his head ruefully. "Don't laugh," he said, trying to make a joke of it. "It's paid for. Besides, the other one is ruined. It'll have to be sent away for new leather straps and padding, and that could take a month or more." He clumped back into the kitchen, explaining in a loud voice as he searched for a cup and a teabag that the simple aluminum peg weighed far less and was much easier to get around on than the heavy prosthetic leg that he usually wore.

When he came back into the room, he poured boiling water from the kettle over the tea bag. Then he placed the cup on the low coffee table to cool and sat on the edge of the sofa. His demeanor changed as he leaned over the unconscious young woman and placed a hand on her pale forehead.

"Who are you?" he whispered softly. "And how in the name of God did you come to be floating around in the ocean, today of all days?"

Though the woman made no sign of having heard or understood his question, Robert continued to gaze at her still features. "Of course, you must know that you're very beautiful," he said after a long pause that was punctuated by the crackling of the fire. "I wonder if your soul is as lovely as your face."

Robert suddenly raised his eyes and saw that I was watching him from my place beside the woodbox, and his face flushed bright with embarrassment. "Don't worry, Meteor, old boy," he assured me. "I know what you must be thinking: finally poor Robert has found a woman he feels comfortable talking to . . . the only catch is that she doesn't even know he's here."

He smiled and looked back down at the silent young woman on the sofa. "But you must admit that it's an intriguing puzzle: behind this angelic face there may lurk the soul of an ax murderer . . . or a saint. And we have no way of knowing which it is."

He raised his eyes again and winked at me.

"But until we have more information, I suppose we'll just have to give her the benefit of the doubt, right?"

I made a small snuffling noise and put my nose between my paws, thinking that the woman was probably none of the things he was imagining, for she looked quite ordinary to me. But then, in those days, I understood very little of how the human mind colors and shapes the ordinary to fit its own conception of reality. And so I could not really appreciate the aura of romance and mystery in which Robert had cloaked his silent guest.

He remained beside the woman until the tea had cooled enough to insure that it would not scald her. Then he cradled her in one arm and spooned a bit of the hot liquid between her slightly parted lips. She swallowed automatically, and he continued to feed her tiny sips of tea and to whisper soft words of praise and encouragement until the cup was empty.

Then he got up and walked to the cottage door to assess the wind once more. Satisfied that it was lessening prior to the arrival of the main storm, he came back into the room and picked the woman up, still wrapped in her blankets. He carried her outside to the Jeep and laid her across the narrow back seat.

The blowing rain had let up a bit as we drove down a narrow rutted track to the abandoned lightkeeper's house and parked in the partial shelter of a paint-peeled wall. Far out on the point of the cape, the lower half of the lighthouse alternately vanished and reappeared among geysers of spray, as huge waves exploded against the black rocks at its base. Robert carefully gauged the intervals of the waves, glancing at his watch from time to time to confirm the number of seconds between sets. He stepped out of the Jeep and gave me a stern look.

"There's an emergency radio out there in the lighthouse that I can use to call the Coast Guard," he said. "I think the wind's down enough now, so they can get a helicopter to us."

He glanced once more at the pale girl on the back seat and reached back to brush his hand across her cheek. "So you sit tight here with Meteor, angel, and I'll try to get you some help."

"Watch over her," he ordered, running his fingers roughly through the damp fur at the back of my neck. "I'll be back in a few minutes."

I whimpered to no avail as he hurried down the overgrown path toward the lighthouse and paused to watch a monstrous set of waves thundering against its base. Then, with snowy cascades of salt foam still pouring from the black rocks, Robert walked quickly across the narrow walkway suspended above the slick stones. When he reached the steel door, he rattled his keys in the lock for a heart-stopping moment. The door creaked open, and he stepped inside an instant before a fresh onslaught of thundering green water slammed into the rocks, enveloping the stout brick lighthouse tower in a wall of cloud and spray.

A short time later, Robert and I stood in the flat clearing that had once been the front yard of the lightkeeper's little house. A clattering roar rose above the fury of the storm as a giant white helicopter skimmed low beneath the scudding clouds and came to a jerky halt above our heads.

A dark figure clad in bulky clothing and wearing a big shiny helmet dropped to our feet on a slender cable and yelled something into Robert's ear. The two men ran to the Jeep. After the other man had looked in upon our poor castaway, he and Robert shouted some more.

Refusing the other man's offer of help, Robert carried the woman in his own weary arms to the center of the yard and laid her in a wire basket that had dropped from the open door of the helicopter.

The helmeted stranger swiftly knelt and strapped her into it. Then he attached the basket to the same cable on which he had descended. Spinning slowly in the whirlwind created by the giant propeller blades, our castaway was drawn up into the belly of the clattering machine. A moment later, the cable was lowered for the last time. The stranger clipped it to his belt, and then he, too, was pulled up into the helicopter.

The man waved at us as the nose of the machine suddenly dropped, and it wheeled away toward the mainland, leaving us alone in the windswept lightkeeper's yard.

We watched the helicopter until it had vanished behind the dunes. Then we returned in the Jeep to Sea Pines Cottage, to await the arrival of the oncoming hurricane.

Chapter 6

AUTUMN

Snug at last within the confines of our sheltered refuge, Robert and I wearily consumed a makeshift meal of canned spaghetti. Then he collapsed on the hearthside sofa to sleep for a while. Retreating to my place by the woodbox, I lay for a long time regarding his haggard features, while I tried to puzzle out the maddening enigma of these human beings. How, I wondered, could the same species that deliberately made wars with the express intention of killing and maiming others of their own kind produce a man like Robert? And were there, as some of the writings he read to me had led me to believe, other men in the world as good as he?

That day I had seen my master abandon his beloved sailing sloop to the merciless sea without so much as a backward glance. Then, twice within a few hours, he had risked his life for another. And though it is a well-known fact that noble canines have often gladly sacrificed life and limb for a beloved mate, a helpless pup or even a kind human master, Robert had repeatedly risked his all for a complete stranger.

I did not understand it then, and I do not pretend to understand it fully now. But the proof I witnessed on that day, that there truly did exist in the world at least one completely selfless human, lit a small spark of kindness that has ever since burned deep within my heart for all of humankind.

Late that night, after a wearying afternoon and an evening spent securing our home as best we could, the hurricane came ashore on Cape Fear, cracking the tops of many of the pine trees in our little forest and driving endless ranks of thundering rollers right up onto the sides of the great sloping dunes.

But the rampaging sea did not reach quite high enough to sweep our snug cottage away, and even the worst of the shrieking winds did not dip quite low enough to seriously breach the protection of our refuge among the dunes.

All night long I watched from the comfort of my blanket on the window seat in Robert's bedroom as the fearsome cyclonic storm hurled everything it had against the beaches of Cape Fear. And though the window casement shook violently, the house shuddered, and at times seemed on the verge of being torn apart by the vicious blows, my heart was filled with happiness. Because once every minute and fifteen seconds throughout that long and terrifying night, the reassuring flash of the Cape Fear light briefly filled the room with its brilliance, reminding me that even in the midst of mortal danger and hardship, my good master had not neglected to attend to his duty of inspecting the generator fuel tanks.

By morning, the storm had gone. We threw open the thick oak door to find a freshly scrubbed blue sky filled with lingering clouds, and the first cool breezes of autumn blew delightful scents of pine and sea salt into our faces.

All around the cottage the forest floor was littered with broken branches from the damaged trees. Robert made a joke of that, telling me that the hurricane had kindly chosen to make its landfall on Cape Fear in order to spare us for many months to come the trouble of going down to the beach to gather driftwood for our fireplace.

Considering the ferocity of the storm, damage to the cottage was relatively light. Though many gray shingles had been torn from the outer walls, only a few broken roof slates lay on the ground, and those were things that could be repaired easily enough.

After a quick breakfast of grilled bacon and toasted bread, Robert got a ladder from the shed, which had lost one of its doors to the storm, and went to work repairing the roof.

Late in the afternoon we finally walked down to look at the beach, which, except for a dark tracing of driftwood and seaweed higher up on the dunes than seemed possible, looked the same as it had before the storm.

We found the battered hull of Robert's beloved sailboat half-buried in the sand near the lighthouse. Her varnished mast was gone, as were the tiller and centerboard, and there was a ragged hole big enough for me to walk through in the planking on her starboard side.

After examining the sad little wreck, Robert said without regret that he thought he might be able to fix her during the coming winter, although we would somehow have to get her back up to the shed first. However, that was work that would have to wait until we had finished repairing the cottage and gathering in the windfall of firewood from the pine forest.

Over the next few weeks, autumn settled firmly over Cape Fear, bringing a new chill to the clear, windy mornings and frosting the tops of the brown sea grasses on many nights. By the time the roof had been made watertight again and new shingles were cut and shaped and nailed to the cottage walls and when the shed door had been replaced and all of the firewood cut and stacked, September was almost over.

As he had done before the hurricane, when our work was finished each evening and our supper had been eaten, Robert huddled over his infernal clacking machine to write while I dreamed beside the fire of chasing rabbits through the pines. And though Robert never again mentioned our pale castaway or the extraordinary events of the stormy day that he had rescued her, I sometimes caught him gazing off into space for long minutes at a time.

On those occasions, I could not help but wonder if he was still pondering the mystery that he had created in his mind about the anonymous young woman who had so briefly touched our lives, then vanished into the sky.

That question was answered for me late one night a few weeks later, when Robert haltingly read aloud the beginnings of a new story that he had been writing. It concerned a beautiful sleeping princess who had fallen under the spell of an evil knight. Eventually, an ugly but kindhearted troll rescued the princess from certain death. But though he was desperately in love with the beautiful princess, the ugly troll could never hope to win her hand.

Even in my humble canine opinion, the foolish story was far from Robert's best work. To make matters worse, it had no ending. When he had finished reading, I politely thumped my tail against the stones of the hearth to show that I had been listening, but secretly I hoped he would put that story away and write something else.

One crisp afternoon after all of our necessary storm repairs were finally completed, we went down to the beach to begin the slow task of digging the wrecked sloop out of the sand. It was difficult and heavy work that promised to go on for several days before we would be able to raise the boat onto her cart and haul her back up to the shed for refitting.

By the time we started back to the cottage, the sun was slipping low over the dunes, and

Robert's denim shirt was stained dark with perspiration from shoveling in the damp sand.

Halfway up the path between the dunes, I stopped to investigate the tracks of a particularly large rabbit that, at least from the tantalizingly fresh smell of its trail, had hopped up into the pine forest just minutes ahead of us.

When I looked up from my sniffing, I was surprised to see Robert standing motionless at the top of the path. He was staring fixedly at something that was hidden from my view by the bulk of the cottage. As I bounded up the path to join him, I spotted a bright red automobile parked on the narrow drive near the front of the cottage.

Immediately, I let out a gruff, noisy bark that was calculated to frighten away any intruder with dirty business on his mind. Then, I raced ahead to investigate the strange car. Vaguely, I heard Robert calling for me to come back, but his voice was strangely low and furtive, and not at all commanding. Refusing to be deterred from my sworn duty to protect my master from Bad Guys, I raced down to the drive while I barked with all my might.

I slid to an ungraceful halt beside the strange car and placed my paws on the sill of the open window. Peering inside, I discovered to my disappointment that the vehicle was empty.

While I still was pondering how the car might have gotten into our drive, I heard a peal of musical laughter behind me, and a lilting voice called out, "Well now, aren't you just about the biggest, meanest watchdog I've ever seen?"

Unused to balancing on hind legs, my attempt to whirl about on the slippery pine needles ended somewhat awkwardly, and I crashed to the ground, my dignity bruised more than my rear end.

Before I could regain my feet, a beautiful young woman wearing dark glasses and a bright green dress was hurrying toward me from the front of the cottage. "Oh, you poor boy," she called sympathetically, "did I startle you?"

I jumped quickly to my feet, prepared to bark again, but it was too late. She was already crouching at my side, running soft fingers through my coat and remarking on its exceptional color and silkiness. Squirming with pleasure at her gentle touch and flattering words, I did not even notice Robert watching us from the deep shadows beside the cottage, until he spoke.

"Is there something I can do for you?" he asked in a neutral tone that was not unpleasant, but not welcoming either.

The beautiful young woman smiled at him. "Oh, I certainly hope so," she said, "because it has taken me weeks to find you. That is," she added, "if you are the keeper of the Cape Fear lighthouse."

She turned slightly toward the top of the towering light which shone beyond the dunes. "I drove down there first, but the little house appears to be abandoned."

Keeping to the shadows, Robert moved a little closer, a puzzled frown darkening his sunburned brow. "I'm the one who looks after the light these days," he replied. "There hasn't been a resident lightkeeper there for many years. It's all largely automated now."

"Ah!" she nodded, as if that somehow explained everything. "Then you are the one I've been looking for."

She beamed Robert a dazzling smile that seemed to brighten the air around her and pushed her dark glasses up onto her forehead, revealing a pair of unforgettable sea-green eyes. "My name is Laura," she said, "and I've come to officially thank you for having saved my life."

Robert stared at her in stunned amazement, and it was clear that he had not suspected until that moment that this beautiful creature might be our poor bedraggled castaway. But then, as you have already seen, neither had I.

"You?" Robert murmured, squinting at the lovely woman standing there on our drive in the rapidly failing light. "You're the one I pulled from the surf?"

"You must think I'm terrible for not coming sooner," Laura apologized, starting toward him with one small hand extended in friendship, "but I was unconscious in a Charlotte hospital for two days after the Coast Guard flew me there. And by the time I came around, no one could remember exactly where I had been found. When my friends finally showed up, they insisted that I return home to Baltimore to recuperate."

She had almost reached the spot where Robert was standing, when I detected the distinctive scent that all humans unconsciously exude when they are terribly frightened.

The fear smell was coming from Robert.

For a moment I did not understand. Even I could see that the beautiful Laura was the sleeping princess from Robert's foolish fairy tale. And now that she had come searching for him, it seemed to provide the perfect happy ending that he had failed to find.

But Robert's eyes had dropped sheepishly to the shadows that were concealing the metal peg he wore. And the reason for his reserve was suddenly clear to me: in his mind, at least, having only one leg made Robert the ugly troll who could never hope to win the hand of the princess, even though she might be eternally grateful for his having saved her life.

Obviously, he feared what Laura would think of him when she saw him as he really was.

Which, of course, was utter nonsense!

As had happened on my very first day with Robert, the instant that I heard Laura's sweet laughter, I had sensed that she was a good and kind human. All of my canine instincts told me that such a person would surely judge Robert by what she saw in his eyes and sensed in his voice, not by counting his legs.

I sensed something else in her, too—something in the way those sea-green eyes gazed into his handsome face told me that Laura had been dreaming about her mysterious rescuer, just as he had been dreaming of her.

But humans are humans and, as I have already explained, they often manage to complicate even the simplest of situations with problems that exist only in their own imaginations.

It was obvious to me, then, that I would have to do something, and do it quickly.

There was an awkward pause as the two young humans stood facing one another across an invisible barrier that separated the late afternoon twilight from the deepening shadows beside the cottage. Laura's slender hand was still raised, waiting for him to take it. Robert's calm gray eyes were clouded with pain and self-doubt as I made my move.

Pretending I had caught the scent of some creature in the forest, I suddenly let out an excited yelp and dashed past Laura, managing to knock her off balance in the process.

That, in turn, obliged Robert either to react and catch her or risk letting her fall to the ground.

My little scheme worked perfectly, for he automatically stepped forward at just the right moment and saved her from the fall. And I happily noted, as he held her in his arms, that he retained his grip for just a moment longer than was absolutely necessary to restore her balance. In that same moment, I also saw Laura glance down at the ugly metal peg he wore. Then she looked straight up into Robert's soft gray eyes with no trace of pity or disgust. And she smiled at him.

"Meteor," Robert scolded me, his handsome features flushed with embarrassment, "you are a very, very bad dog!"

Of course, I dropped my tail between my legs and managed to look ashamed. But I could tell from the tone of Robert's voice that he had only said what was expected of him in that situation.

And so, I naively allowed myself to believe, I had easily put aside all of Robert's foolish notions about princesses and trolls.

Chapter 7

LAURA AND ROBERT

The sheer power of a man and a woman touching, however briefly, can never be overestimated.

The small intimacy of their quick embrace outside the cottage had the effect of releasing pent up torrents of conversation from the two young humans. Robert clumsily apologized to Laura for my rude behavior, saying he couldn't understand what had gotten into me. Then he stammered out a second apology for not having initially greeted her with more warmth, and he blamed his surprise at her sudden appearance for his poor manners.

Laura laughed delightedly and forgave both of us, then she asked how I had come to be named Meteor. Robert promised to tell her that story. But first he said he just had to know how she had ended up in the sea off our beach on the day of the storm.

As darkness closed in around Cape Fear that night, the three of us lounged before the fireplace with the delicious aroma of a savory fish chowder wafting from the cauldron.

Robert and Laura sipped glasses of chilled white

wine on the sofa, while dozens of excited questions flew between them. And all the while, green eyes and gray ones were flashing subtle messages faster than words could be spoken.

Though she was neither princess nor angel, or any of the other things that Robert had imagined her to be, Laura's quick wit, obvious intelligence and determined spirit captivated him more surely than any fairy-tale whimsy that he might have been entertaining in his daydreams.

She was, Laura replied to his most anxious questions, a secretary in a large Baltimore manufacturing company. But that, she hastened to add, was only temporary. Her green eyes sparked with passion as she explained that she was really an artist: a pretty good sculptor and an even better potter. She had been attending university classes at night and saving her money against the day when she had enough to quit her job and give herself a year to test her talent.

On the day that we found her, she had been returning from Florida aboard a large power yacht owned by the wealthy father of a young man whom she evasively described as an old friend, but her voice told me he was more than that.

The sailing trip had been her first vacation since leaving school. But three days out of St. Augustine, the leisurely cruise had turned into a nightmare, when the distant hurricane had unexpectedly veered north. Her friend had spent the next two days desperately trying to outrun the storm in increasingly high winds and towering seas.

It was late at night, and they had just spotted

the comforting beacon of the Cape Fear light, when Laura had been swept overboard by a huge wave.

She had floated in the cold, storm-tossed Atlantic all of that night and half of the next day before Robert had rescued her. Her distraught friend, meanwhile, had guided the battered yacht to the safety of a protected harbor farther up the coast at New Bern, certain that she had been drowned.

Laura suddenly shivered in the evening chill, and Robert leaped up to place another log on the fire. Then, at her insistence, he briefly related the circumstances of her rescue. To my great dismay, he minimized his heroism to the point where it seemed as if he had done no more than toss a life ring out into the waves and pull her in.

Laura, however, would have none of his false modesty. For, in her tireless quest to track him down, she had learned of his earlier heroism as an army medic in the war: heroism that had ended with Robert sacrificing himself in an attempt to save other men. My pride in my master was boosted even higher that night, as I learned for the first time that Robert's selfless act had earned him the highest decoration for valor that his country could bestow.

Laura knew also, from the Coast Guard helicopter pilot whom she had finally located a few days before, that Robert's dash to reach the emergency radio in the storm-besieged lighthouse had, in itself, been an act of supreme courage.

Robert blushed like a schoolboy when she had finished relating that information and replied that he only did what anyone would have done under the circumstances.

They talked for hours after that, telling one another the stories of their lives, revealing their likes and dislikes, laughing over old songs they had both sung as children, and discussing an obscure book that both had recently read.

At some point, I must have fallen asleep. For when next I raised my head, the conversation had waned and the fire had burned down to a mound of glowing embers.

I looked around in the dim light and saw that they were still on the sofa, their faces nearly touching. Laura's arms were lightly resting on Robert's shoulders, and her lovely sea-green eyes gazed somberly into his gray ones.

I watched their lips touch. And, though I do not pretend to understand that particular expression of human courting behavior, I felt a lump rise into my throat at the tenderness of the moment. It seemed painfully obvious to me that the Maker in His great wisdom had brought Robert and Laura together.

The moon was high as they walked outside to the bright red automobile a short time later. When Laura was seated in the car, Robert leaned in through the open window and spoke so softly to her that I could not hear his words.

Energized by the cool night air and the successful role that I had played in bringing the young lovers together, I happily ran off into the forest, hoping to scare up a prowling raccoon that lately had been foraging around the shed.

Minutes later, I heard the engine of Laura's

car starting. I broke off my wanderings and returned to find Robert watching its lights growing smaller and smaller among the dunes.

Then he turned and limped slowly up to the cottage on his one good leg and his metal peg, and I had the feeling that something was not right.

Later that night, as I lay on my blanket in the upstairs window seat, Robert sat against the pillows on his bed and stared gloomily at the enchantingly moonlit seascape behind me. "Meteor," he suddenly said from the darkness, "I think that I am falling in love with her, and I do not know what to do about it, for she has told me that another man wishes to marry her. He is wealthy and handsome and will give her everything she could ever desire."

I snorted contemptuously, wishing for once that I had the power of human speech, so that I could tell my foolish master that he had fallen in love with Laura on the day he pulled her from the sea. I would also have told him in no uncertain terms what I thought he should do, because I had read in her eyes that Laura was in love with him, and no other.

But I am only a dog, and so I could do nothing but sigh heavily from my blanket.

"The thing is," Robert said—though this time I believe that he was attempting to convince himself and not me—"she is so beautiful, so perfect in every way . . . while I . . ."

His voice trailed off, and in the darkness I knew that he was looking down at the flat place on the blankets where the shape of his missing leg should have been.

"She deserves so much more than this," he said with finality.

To my great surprise, I found myself in resentful agreement with Robert's last statement.

Oh, what I would have given at that moment if I could have raised my head and opened my mouth and shouted, "Yes! Yes, you great oafish human, you are right. Laura does deserve more, much more than your blind self-pity will permit her to have."

I closed my eyes and tried to think about chasing rabbits through the pine forest, which is something that has always calmed me when I am upset.

Chapter 8

LOVESTRUCK

I think that there may be no creature in this world as unhappy as a lovestruck human who has been deprived of the object of that love.

No matter that Robert's love was plainly and warmly reciprocated by Laura. No matter that it was he himself who had sent her away into the night. The foolish man was beside himself with grief and longing.

The next day it rained, and so we did not go down to the beach as usual. Instead, Robert hovered about the cottage like a wraith, alternately sitting before his typing machine to clack out a few words, then abruptly ripping the sheet of paper from its rollers and hurling it in a crumpled ball to the floor, before getting up to pace and mutter to himself.

I found his behavior maddening.

When at last he let me outside to do my business, I dashed off into the dripping pine forest and did not return for many hours, preferring the cold and wet discomforts of the natural world to the manufactured gloom that had suddenly invaded our warm retreat.

As I halfheartedly scratched at the muddy entrance to a hidden rabbit burrow—a chance discovery that only the day before would have filled my heart with gladness—I wondered exactly what Robert said to Laura as he had stood by her car the night before. I wondered, too, why she had not come back, despite his words.

Laura had impressed me as a person who was altogether far more sensible and tenacious than my lovestruck master and one who would not so easily give up what she wanted.

I thought that perhaps I had been wrong about her love for him.

I had expected far more of a fight from her.

⚜

For three days it rained.

And for three days Robert's mood grew darker and more somber.

Then, finally, the blessed sun came out again, steaming the moisture out of the pine forest and the gray shingles of the cottage. And so we returned to the beach to resume digging the wrecked sailboat from the sand.

I shall never forget the look on Robert's face as we marched down the beach that morning and spied the jaunty little blue tent pitched atop a tall dune overlooking the site of the buried boat. A tiny white pennant with a little red heart in its center fluttered above the tent as we made our way along the damp shore, causing Robert to scowl and shake his head.

"Now what kind of fool would pitch a tent way up there?" he wondered aloud as we neared the boat.

His question was answered as Laura's head popped up from behind the buried hull. She raised a colorful bandana to dab at the drops of perspiration beaded on her forehead, then frowned at the pair of us.

"Well, it's about time you two showed up," she called. "I was beginning to believe that I was going to have to dig this boat out of here all by myself."

Robert's mouth fell open as he walked around to where she knelt and saw that she had already freed the entire port side of the sailboat from the sand.

"Laura!" he gasped when he had regained his wits. "What are you doing here?"

"Well, it certainly isn't brain surgery," she laughed, proudly regarding the results of her labor. "But I do believe that your boat is now nearly ready to be removed from this hole before it caves in again . . . this sand is terrible about falling back into holes."

He sat weakly on the edge of the upraised gunwale and stared at her. "You said you were going back to Baltimore," he began.

Laura nodded. "And I did go back. Then I quit my job and gathered up everything that I owned, and here I am." She grinned mischievously and inclined her head down the beach. "My car is parked there by the lighthouse, with a U-Haul trailer attached. . . . I hope you've got lots of room, because I brought my potter's wheel and my small kiln. . . . Of course, we'll have to build a new one for the larger pieces I want to throw . . ."

"But I thought we had agreed the other night . . ." he protested helplessly.

Laura climbed out of the hole, brushing the sand off her hands, and came around to rest them on his shoulders.

"Ah yes, that," she said, regarding him seriously. "We did not *agree*, Robert. You *told* me to forget that we had ever met. You also advised me to return to Baltimore to a man I *don't* love."

She leaned close to him and smiled. "I guess you'll just have to console yourself with the knowledge that at least I took part of your advice. I did return to Baltimore."

Robert shook his head, bewildered. "This is impossible," he muttered, lowering his eyes to that damned peg leg. "You can't imagine what . . . what it would be like with . . . a man like me. . . ."

Laura straightened and regarded him for a long moment. It was clear that she knew exactly what he meant.

"Perhaps you're right," she said finally. "I can't really imagine what it would be like. So I suppose I shall just have to find that out for myself."

Robert shook his head abruptly. "No," he said, horrified. "I couldn't . . . allow that. Not ever! I don't even want to discuss it."

Laura put her hands on her hips and stood there looking at him for a moment longer. Then she bent and softly kissed his lips.

"Very well, Robert," she said. "We won't discuss it. However, as long as I've gone to all of this trouble, shall we get your boat out of that hole now? After all," she added, "it's really my fault that it's there in the first place."

They worked for the remainder of that strange day, scooping out the wet sand that had gathered inside the hull, and then bringing the wheeled cart attached to the hitch on the back of the Jeep and pulling the boat up onto the cart with the winch. And, as I watched them struggling together, I knew in my heart that I had been right about Laura and Robert.

They were truly meant for each other.

But there was still the problem of Robert's foolish notions about his disfigurement and perhaps even his worthiness as a man and Laura's mate.

Time, I told myself. Time and Laura's gentle persistence would gradually overcome his fears and objections.

But, as is usual whenever I attempt to predict what humans will do, I was wrong again.

Chapter 9

TRESPASSER

That night, with the hull of the sailboat safely stowed in the shed, the three of us wearily retired to the familiar warmth of the cottage to eat a slapdash supper of cold sandwiches and hot soup from cans. Robert and Laura had not spoken again of her intentions, although I could see that Robert was growing more and more uneasy in anticipation of their next confrontation.

As the supper things were cleared away, I warily retreated to my place by the woodbox and waited anxiously for the inevitable clash of wills.

To my surprise, Laura came out of the kitchen, tossed her warm coat over her shoulders and announced that she was retiring to her tent on the dunes.

"That's ridiculous!" Robert spluttered. "You can't stay out there all alone. "Besides," he added, "it's likely to get quite cold tonight."

Smiling sweetly, she kissed his red face and started for the door. "I can and I will stay there," she informed him. "And it will please you to know that I have a very expensive down sleeping bag to keep me warm," a short pause and then, "since you will not."

And with that she was gone out the door.

Oh, how my master paced and fumed when she was gone, shouting to the big stuffed fish on the wall about what a damned stubborn and exasperating woman she was, and telling me how glad he was that he had refused to have anything more to do with her. Then, almost in the same breath with which he had been berating her bullheadedness, he hurried to the window and peered worriedly out into the darkness, in hopes of spotting her on the path.

Later, Robert sat propped against the pillows on his bed and gazed out morosely at the seascape beyond my window, his eyes fixed on the glow of the lantern that shone like a tiny beacon atop the dune where Laura had pitched her tent. He muttered darkly to himself until the small light was extinguished.

I kept vigil over his restless sleep and watched the whitecaps on the sea turn iridescent in the moonlight. My keen hunter's ears heard shuffling from below, and I turned at the sound of stealthy footsteps on the stairs. My muscles tensed as I watched the bedroom door open slowly.

I leaped off my blanket, prepared to lunge at the intruder, when a wavering light filled the bedroom, and I saw Laura standing in the doorway with a candle in her hand.

Laura raised a finger to her lips, begging me for silence. I watched as she glided silently to the bed and gently lifted the comforter from Robert's body.

She stood there gazing down for several minutes, her lovely features in the candlelight cast into an expression of profound sadness at what the Bad Guys had done to our poor Robert. Then she allowed her heavy coat to slip to the floor, revealing the girlish silhouette of her slender body.

Placing the flickering candle on the nightstand, Laura softly slipped into Robert's bed. He stirred, then opened his eyes and started to speak.

"Hush, my darling," Laura whispered, placing a small hand over his lips to still his protest. "For I have already seen all that you forbade me to see, and it has not changed a thing. I love only you, Robert. I want to be with you and no other."

Without warning, my master began to weep, placing his cheek on her soft breast and sobbing so deeply that I feared his great heart might burst with the emotions he was experiencing. "I have been such a damned fool," he said between gasps. "I will never again mistrust your judgment."

I do not know what happened between them after that, for the moment was far too private for me to remain there any longer. Quietly I trotted to the stairs, and for the first time since I had come to Sea Pines Cottage, I spent a night alone in my warm place by the hearth.

Laura did not leave Robert's side that night, nor any other.

And so there were two of us to watch over him.

Chapter 10

WE THREE

Were any creatures ever happier on this earth than the three of us in that magical autumn? I could not then have imagined that any greater joy was possible.

We were golden beings tramping the pristine beaches and wandering the pine forest in the clean crisp air, bringing home little harvests of berries and fish and wild pumpkins to supplement our larder, laying in supplies and tightening the creaking old cottage against the ravages of the winter soon to come, or laughing and splashing like children as we hunted for scuttling crabs in the chilly tidal pools among the rocks.

Soon our lives had settled into an ideal pattern of busy days of work and play. Each evening we all went down to the lighthouse, while Robert attended his keeper's duties. Then we would return home to meals which, especially on Laura's cooking days, seemed somehow far more delicious than their plain ingredients could rightly justify.

During that time, the big main room of the cottage was rearranged to accommodate Laura's pottery wheel as well as a big gasoline generator to power it and the lights she needed for her work. When supper was done, the sound of her soft singing as she formed wondrously curved objects from ordinary gray clay overlaid the clacking of Robert's typing machine, making even that onerous noise sound somehow contented and natural.

And, at the end of every evening, Robert would examine what she had created with her hands, and Laura would read the pages that he had written. Then each would evaluate the other's work with loving regard, while they sat before the fire with their mugs of chocolate or coffee.

For me, basking in the glow of Robert and Laura's extraordinary devotion and thriving on those culinary masterpieces, life had become sheer heaven.

Late November brought an early winter and, with it, great blue Arctic northers that howled around the eaves of our snug cottage for days on end. But extra logs on the fire kept us all warm and cozy, and we had little need to venture outside.

On the anniversary of my arrival at Sea Pines Cottage, Robert and Laura left me to guard our home and went off to Thunderbolt. I was slightly jealous at being left behind, but now I had ample time to chase the rabbit I'd been stalking for days.

I heard the rumble of the Jeep long before it appeared over the rise from the dunes. It churned up dust as Robert brought it to a stop in front of our dingy gray home. Laura's musical laugh accompanied the unloading of the many packages that were then carried into the house. Before I could find out what was in the countless bags and boxes, Robert hailed me to the front door.

"Come on boy, we've been ordered to gather some greenery," he said, as he gave Laura a sly smile and a kiss.

The tarp we dragged back home was filled with pine branches, holly branches laden with red berries, terrible tasting berries, I might add, and pinecones.

I sat next to Laura as she connected the pine branches to each other with small pieces of green fuzzy wire, pipe cleaners she called them, and created garlands that Robert put on the fireplace mantle and draped around the outside of the front door. Laura put them on the windowsill as she added shiny apples from one of the boxes, for just a touch of red, she said. She nestled candles and pinecones in as well.

We had brought the smell of my beloved piney forest into the house, and it was heavenly. As darkness fell that evening, Laura systematically walked around the house as she turned on the lights she had intertwined with the pine boughs.

As she stood in the middle of the room and turned around to enjoy her handiwork, Laura said that there was something else she wanted to do. She went to a small cupboard near the fireplace and took out a pottery piece she had made for the occasion. It was a dark green candle holder that had a finger loop on the side decorated with holly leaves and berries. With Robert and me watching, Laura put a tall white candle in the holder and placed it on the window sill and lit it.

"So strangers know they are welcome," she smiled.

Before starting the evening meal, Laura took the bow that had been around my neck the previous year from the hook where Robert had left it and tied it around a bunch of strange-looking greens with little white berries that she said would make me sick. She put a small rubber object under the open kitchen door, then stood on a chair and attached the beribboned twigs to a nail right in the center of the doorway. Getting down off the chair, she looked up at the small decoration and smiled.

"This is a magical plant, Meteor. When two people meet under the mistletoe, they kiss, just like magic." With that explanation, she leaned down and kissed my muzzle. "See, it's magic," she said and she giggled, a musical sound that I loved to hear.

Periodically during the next few weeks, every time Robert and Laura walked under the little branches, they would kiss, and so, like many things that happened that day, mistletoe became a Christmas tradition at Sea Pines Cottage.

After dinner the three of us sat curled up on the sofa, and I looked around the room. In the dim light of only the fire and Christmas lights, it reminded me of being outside on a bright starlit night and seeing the stars through the branches of the trees. It really was quite magical.

Two weeks later, Robert came in with a tree

that he had cut from the far reaches of the small pine forest that surrounded our home. After arranging it in a pot that allowed it to stand upright in the house, Laura wrapped strings and strings of lights, popcorn (which she shared with me), and cranberries—which were not particularly tasty. She added shiny balls from the remaining boxes of their shopping trip.

Once again, magic filled the air as tiny lights and candles warmed the house even without the fireplace which, of course, was always burning this time of year. When the lights on the tree came on, the room was transformed into a wonderland.

Christmas had come to Sea Pines Cottage.

❧❧❧❧

The young lovers welcomed the confining gloom of the gray days and racing storm clouds, for they were then able to devote all of their time to their respective arts and to one another. During that period, their love blossomed; and their art, so they each claimed, was vastly improved. But before winter had the chance to set in and keep us bound to our island, the young lovers took a trip.

❧❧❧❧

Robert and Laura went to Baltimore to be married the day before Christmas. Robert had a new blue suit, and his repaired prosthetic leg was now fitted out with a shiny black shoe that,

Laura insisted, made his disability practically un-
noticeable to anyone who did not already know of
it.

If he disbelieved her, he did not say so.

After the wedding, they traveled to New York,
where Robert met with a publisher who had expressed an interest in putting some of his writings into books and where Laura was anxious to
visit galleries that might be interested in showing her work.

While they were away, I was sent off to Sam
Wilson's place on the mainland, where I resided
in the kennels with the other gun dogs that he
bred and trained.

It was a visit that I had dreaded, for the sting
of my disgrace as a hunter remained fresh in my
mind then and I still sometimes thought long-
ingly of dimly recalled carefree days with my
mother and my siblings, and of the great breed
championships that were forever denied to me.

To my great surprise, however, when I arrived
at Sam Wilson's farm, I alone seemed to remember or care that I had once failed as a hunting dog.

Even more astonishing, the kennels were not
at all as I had remembered them from my pup-
pyhood. Now, cold, drab runs of concrete and
wire housed even Sam Wilson's most honored
champions.

I could discover no sense of warmth or joy or
hope, either in the steel bowls of tasteless kibble
served once a day or in the constant confine-
ment of the nervous, high-strung setters and retrievers who spent the endless hours between

hunts and training sessions simply longing for a kind word from their human keepers or a romp in the surrounding woods.

By the time that Robert and Laura returned to take me home, I had come to realize that my life at Sea Pines Cottage was far richer and fuller than any that those sad, groomed hunting champions could ever dream of.

And I thanked the Maker again for having given me Robert, and now Laura, to watch over and to serve.

$$\sim\!\!\infty\!\!\infty\!\!\sim$$

Winter turned to spring and then to summer again, and Robert's writings began to be printed in books and magazines. Cars would occasionally be driven along the long sandy road across the dunes and carried humans to Sea Pines Cottage just to admire and purchase Laura's beautiful pottery.

Before long, the maturing of their artistic careers began to bring in money that was used to enlarge the shed into a proper studio for Laura's sculpting and a room to display her work.

Although we also added a few modern conveniences to the house and bought a newer, more reliable Jeep, little else changed at Sea Pines Cottage.

We three still wandered the pine forest together in search of berries, mushrooms or whatever other bounty the particular season might produce. And that summer the newly refurbished sailboat was relaunched. Robert wanted to christen it *The Laura,* but the real Laura balked at the idea and suggested *Kismet* would be more appropriate, since fate had brought them together. She reached down and rubbed my ears and said, "All three of us." So the *Kismet* she became, and she provided us afterwards with months of cruising pleasure and a steady supply of fresh fish.

Sea Pines Cottage seemed always to be alive with the sounds of laughter and the warm glow of love.

We three might have gone on that way forever.

But, as I have come to learn in the course of time, nothing remains constant. And so our well-ordered lives underwent another incredible change, just as we had gotten comfortable with the new ways.

Chapter 11

NICHOLAS

A tiny, squalling, red-faced intruder invaded our quiet sanctuary on Christmas Eve, the first anniversary of Laura and Robert's marriage.

Born in the big iron bed overlooking the untamed sea and the Cape Fear light, the little fellow was ushered into the world with the assistance of Laura's crab-faced Aunt Mazie.

Mazie, a wizened little nurse with a good heart and a snappish temper, had arrived on the train from Baltimore a few days earlier. First off, she had the sheer audacity to demand that I be banished permanently to the shed, in order, she said, to protect both mother and child against a host of unspecified diseases that she believed were carried by dogs.

I cannot say that I cared at all for that woman.

Robert and Laura, of course, refused to consider removing me from my rightful post as guardian of the household. I was, however, temporarily restricted to the immediate vicinity of the fireplace and strongly cautioned against growling at Aunt Mazie, no matter how unreasonable she became.

So I did not, unfortunately, actually witness the birth of little Nicholas.

But I did hear his first lusty bellow of life racketing down the stairwell as I anxiously kept watch beneath the cheerful greenery and Christmas stockings hung from the blackened mantelpiece.

And I was the one who was there to lick Robert's hand in joyous congratulation as he stumbled into the main room moments later with a huge smile lighting his handsome features.

"A son, Meteor! We have a beautiful, healthy son," he told me in a voice tremulous with the miracle that he had just witnessed. "You must always watch over him and care for him," he said, running his strong fingers over the favorite place at the back of my neck.

Then my good master gazed at the smoke rising up through the old stone chimney to the heavens, and his tone became fervent. "No harm must ever come to him," he humbly beseeched the Maker above. "Please."

I touched my nose to Robert's hand to let him know that he could depend on me to lay down my life for little Nicholas, just as I would gladly do for our beloved Laura and himself. And I believe, in that solemn moment, that Robert understood my meaning exactly. For when his prayer was done, he smiled and massaged my neck all the harder.

Then he went to the peg by the door and took down his coat. The two of us walked out under a clear, starry sky to stroll along the beach and watch the brilliant meteors falling into the cold sea.

***

Little Nicholas! Born with a smile of delight upon his lips, the son of Robert and Laura was every bit as strong and as beautiful as Robert had claimed, a charming cherub with his mother's sea-green eyes and his father's thick dark hair and robust physique.

From the moment of his arrival at Sea Pines Cottage, Nicholas captivated us all with that angelic smile and a sweet cooing babble. And very soon his every wish became our command.

Within a week, thankfully, Aunt Mazie departed, leaving our little family alone to look after the newborn princeling. And look after him we did, dashing long-accustomed schedules and familiar habits to attend his midnight feedings, creeping silently through the house to avoid disturbing his frequent naps, or driving late at night into Thunderbolt to obtain special drops for his upset tummy.

Though he ruled us all with an iron will, Nicholas rewarded us well for our faithful service to him, dispensing sunny smiles and great slobbering kisses on a regular basis and always burping loudly and appreciatively after each and every meal.

Within six weeks, Nicholas was basking beside me on a knitted throw before the hearth.

Within six months, he was tangling his strong little fingers in my coat and making serious grabs for my carelessly lolling tongue.

By the time another span of seasons had passed and he was a year old, Nicholas had christened me Mee-Yor—his first real word—and he was following me around the cottage on chubby little legs.

I had never known such bliss.

❦

And so the seasons sped by at Sea Pines Cottage, with little Nicholas growing stronger and straighter each year, and all of us happier and more contented than we had ever been.

Soon the baby had become a little boy. His clumsy fingers that gripped my ears gave over to loving fingers that rubbed my favorite spot, and then to sure little hands whose solemn duty it had become to fill my food bowl to overflowing, to smuggle forbidden treats to me from the dinner table, and to pick the clinging sandspurs from my long, silky coat.

Together, we ran on the beach in summer and chased rabbits through the autumn forest and climbed the lighthouse tower to watch the ever changing moods of the wintry sea. I always remembered the charge that Robert had given me on the night that Nicholas was born; and always I was prepared to lay down my life for that wondrous child and would have done so without an instant's hesitation or remorse.

All the while that Nicholas was growing and delighting us, Robert and Laura were growing too. But their growth was of a different kind, expressed in their ever-expanding love for one another, their confidence in their art and themselves, and in the joy that they discovered afresh at the beginning of each new day.

As the years went by, Robert became an important writer who, under Laura's careful management of contracts and royalties and such, was paid more and more money for his books. Laura's work, too, had begun to command serious respect in the art world and was appearing in the inventories of important New York galleries.

Their growing prosperity was directed at remodeling Sea Pines Cottage into a large, modern home with all of the comforts that electricity and proper insulation and a paved road up from the dunes could provide.

The old place sprouted a new wing of glass and wood and open balconies that was more than twice as large as the original fisherman's dwelling. And the old part of the building was rewired, repainted and reshingled nearly beyond recognition.

But the essential things did not change.

The blackened hearth and the big main room remained largely untouched. Robert continued to do his writing there on the clacking old typing machine. The large room was where the family always gathered at the end of each day.

Robert and Laura continued to sleep in the old upstairs bedroom with its breathtaking view of the sea, though I spent my nights at the foot of the bed in Nicholas' room down the hall.

In fine weather, we sailed our little sloop *Kismet* out beyond the breakers to fish and cruise or laze in the sun. And, every day without fail, we all trekked down to the Cape Fear lighthouse to monitor the generator tanks and climb the winding stairs to oil the ceaselessly turning bearings and gears of the great rotating beacon.

Again, I came to believe that no greater happiness could ever be given to any creatures than that which we enjoyed.

I deluded myself into believing that such happiness was an endless condition of our existence.

It took one singular event to shake me out of my complacency and to demonstrate vividly that danger is always lurking where you least expect to find it.

Chapter 12

BAD GUYS

Although looking after my little family absorbed a great portion of my time, not every waking moment was devoted to duty. While he was still a tyke, Nicholas took long afternoon naps daily. And, later, when he was a bit older, the boy began traveling to the school in nearby Thunderbolt. During those daytime respites from attending the constant needs of the small child, Laura often worked in her studio, while Robert sat clacking away at his writing machine or thinking about one of his stories before the fireplace in the big main room.

At such times I was free to roam the pine forest, beach and the great salt marsh, though I seldom strayed out of earshot of Robert's sharp whistling summons. But since my hearing was, in those days, extremely acute, the range of Robert's shrill whistle encompassed a large portion of the island.

As much as I loved my little family and the rough attentions of little Nicholas, I must confess that I always savored those solitary tramps into the wild. And often I made discoveries that my humans might have overlooked entirely, had I not later led them to my finds.

Such was the case one sunny spring morning when I chanced upon a large wooden box washed up upon the sands. Though the weed-draped object smelled no different to me from any other piece of flotsam, the sudden appearance of the crate, intact and unopened, on our beach seemed to demand human attention. So, of course, I immediately ran back to the cottage and dragged my master down to the water's edge to investigate.

After Robert had pried it open, to his great delight, the crate contained boxes and boxes of fine Havana cigars, and each fragrant cylinder of rich, hand-rolled tobacco was perfectly preserved in its own slim watertight tube of shiny metal.

Since there had been a great storm at sea only a day or two before, Robert speculated that the booty must have been swept from the deck of a passing freighter. On the other hand, he later fretted as he touched a flame to the first brown stick and let the thick blue smoke swirl about his handsome face, what kind of captain would carry such expensive and forbidden cargo on an open deck? Maybe the ship had gone down in the storm. Or, as it seemed far more likely, perhaps the contraband cigars had fallen into the sea while being transferred into the smaller boat of some furtive coastal smuggler.

Altogether, it was a delicious and insoluble mystery that added immensely to Robert's enjoyment of the exotic smokes, as well as to my own role as the hero of the hour. Had it not been for my diligence in fetching him to the scene, Robert bragged to Laura, the treasure would surely have been carried back out to sea on the following tide.

So I glowed in the lavish praise of my master for having found what came to be known in family lore as "Meteor's treasure chest." And even though Laura laughingly, but firmly, forbade him to light one of the pungent cigars—which she insisted on labeling "stinking weeds"—inside the cottage, after every storm at sea for years thereafter, Robert would laughingly suggest that I take a run on the beach to see if any more "treasure" could be found.

This is not to say that all of my solitary discoveries were quite as fortuitous or as pleasing to my family as that one had been. On one unhappy occasion the following summer, for instance, I chanced upon an agitated mother skunk near the seaward edge of the pine forest some distance from the cottage. Though I meant her no harm as I charged into the small thicket where she had made her den, the striped mother skunk wrongly interpreted my good-natured barking as a threat to her litter of newborn kits and liberally doused me with the truly horrible perfume that is uniquely skunk.

So bad did I smell following the encounter that, even after I had endured three successive baths in a big tub of sudsy water behind the shed, not even my beloved Nicholas could bear my presence. Like one of Robert's foul Havana cigars, I was banished for days from the cottage and my favorite fireside nook. Since I was made cautious by that bitter experience, my subsequent forays into the wild were somewhat less exuberant, though they were no less enjoyable than before.

As the seasons passed, my explorations often led me to the secret nesting places and hideaways of the many creatures that shared our little island. From such chance encounters, I came to recognize and respect the signs of impending trouble that a number of our wild neighbors display when they feel threatened. From hard experience, I learned that the bristling quills of the porcupine, the sibilant hiss of the cottonmouth and the low growl of the bobcat are all unmistakable warnings to stay clear. In time I came to understand that those creatures the Maker did not equip well to flee from danger, like the rabbit and the deer, or to hide like the mole and the field mouse, He gave the protection of the sting and the bite . . . and the horrible perfume.

Even more than my highly praised discovery of the mysterious box, I now believe, those lessons in caution benefited my human family, because Robert and Laura and little Nicholas often tramped the wilds together. Though they frequently laughed at my sudden frantic forays into the trees and were convinced, I am certain, that I was always racing off in pursuit of another elusive rabbit, that was never entirely true. While no true canine is immune to the intoxicating lure of a fresh trail, many of my noisy charges ahead of the family were intended to warn of hidden dangers on the path ahead. Despite the fact that my well-intentioned actions were often misunderstood, I loved my humans more than life itself and never once resented the laughter that implied I was a foolish and comical creature.

In the end, I think, any such sentiments that my family might have harbored toward me were largely put to rest the day the hunters came.

It happened on a dreary February afternoon in the year that Nicholas first started going to school. The rough road across the dunes to the causeway had been newly improved that summer. Each school-day morning, a great yellow bus rumbled out from the mainland to transport the boy to his teachers. After an interminable span of hours, the bus always returned him to the same spot at the end of our drive, where I would be breathlessly waiting to lavish attention upon him and to receive whatever small treat he had saved for me from his little lunch box.

On that particular day, I had wandered farther than usual into the salt marsh that covers much of the island. As I snuffled along a frost-rimed deer trail with the sharp, musky scent of raccoon wafting deliciously into my nose, I was enjoying the cold, clean air and keeping an ear tuned for the distinctive sound of the yellow school bus. According to the sluggish track of the cloud-dulled sun across the wintry sky, the big machine would soon come rumbling across the marsh to the dunes, which would be my signal to race home to meet Nicholas.

I had just paused to mark my territory at the

base of a spindly pine, while I was idly thinking about how nice it would be to lick my boy's small, warm face and tumble with him in the dry grass before the cottage stoop, when I heard men talking in low, furtive tones.

The sound of human voices in that isolated spot did not immediately alarm me. For though our island had no other permanent residents, visitors often came to view and photograph the many sea birds and other wild creatures in the protected wetlands. Remembering the frightening story of the Bad Guys who had once caused Robert such pain, I liked to investigate all strangers, to be certain that they posed no threat to Sea Pines Cottage or any of its residents.

I trotted toward the sound of the voices with my tail wagging, prepared to issue a friendly greeting and, perhaps, receive a pat on the head as I covertly sniffed the visitors for some hint of their intentions.

My first sight of these strangers, however, was not at all reassuring.

The two men were huddled in a makeshift blind constructed of cut saplings that they had lashed together and covered with dry reeds. I could see by the mottled green fabric of their clothes—like the clothes that had been worn by most of the men who came to Sam Wilson's kennels—that they were hunters. The small metal boat that had been dragged up onto the mud bank behind the men told me they had paddled across open water from the boat ramp on the far side of the salt marsh.

I halted in a tangle of brush a dozen steps or so from the two men, reluctant to go any closer.

At that range, I could clearly see the dull gleam of light on the oiled barrels of the deadly rifles that protruded through the little opening in the front of their blind.

As I stood silently watching from one side, a flask was passed between the men. I smelled the raw, sickening odor of cheap whiskey and heard them arguing in slurred voices about whether this was the same spot where they had shot and killed a deer some years before.

All the old memories of thundering guns and the uncontrollable terror that had remained tucked away in a dark recess of my heart and mind for so long came racing back to me with paralyzing suddenness. My fears were instantly redoubled, as both hunters turned at the sound of some small animal rummaging innocently through the brush in front of their blind. Before my horrified eyes, the men lifted their guns simultaneously. The flat, metallic clunk of high powered bullets being loaded into firing chambers rang through the cold, damp air as they prepared to fire blindly at whatever hapless creature had made the sounds they had heard.

I was at the point of turning and fleeing for home, when, far off in the distance, I detected the faint drone of the school bus grinding its way toward the marsh. In that instant, my blood turned to ice. I realized that the drunken hunters had situated their blind directly facing the nearby road—thickly screened by brush and reeds—down which, in a few short moments, Nicholas and his schoolmates would be riding.

I had a quick, horrible vision of steel-jacketed

deer slugs ripping through the flimsy side of the yellow bus and into the tender cargo it carried.

Then something happened to me. It was something that I was as helpless to explain that day as the unreasoning terror of guns and gunfire that had so long ago ended my career as a hunting dog. Mute with fear, every thought but the unthinkable image of the school bus riddled with bullet holes banished from my fear-numbed brain, I sprang forward and crashed noisily through the reeds, racing head-on for the hunters' blind.

Dimly, I recall seeing the men's dull, murderous eyes shifting toward the unexpected racket of my charge. Though I must have seen the bright yellow tongues of fire leaping from the muzzles of their weapons as well and heard the deafening reports of their badly aimed shots, I remember nothing of that.

In less than a heartbeat, I was upon them, snarling and ripping at the green camouflage of a begrimed sleeve, and whirling to snap viciously at a thickly padded buttock.

Vaguely, I heard the school bus passing by on the road a hundred yards away. Then a mud-encrusted boot thumped into the side of my head; and I rolled away with a yelp and splashed heavily into the freezing marsh water with a loud ringing in my ears.

Clambering up onto the slick, freezing bank, I barely escaped into the cover of the reeds, ahead of another thunderous volley of angry rifle shots.

I painfully limped back to the refuge of Sea

Pines Cottage in the failing afternoon light, barely able to walk. There was a burning tear in my right side where I had crashed into the spear-sharp stump of one of the saplings that the hunters had cut, and my vision was blurred with blood from the jagged, seeping wound on my head.

As I slowly dragged myself toward home, I wondered what would become of me. For though I had at last conquered my fear of guns and gunfire that had disgraced me as a member of my breed, I had also violated that most sacred rule of all canine behavior: I had attacked a man—two men.

Lowering my head and gritting my teeth against the stabbing pain in my side, I staggered with painful deliberateness toward home and whatever fate might await me there. As I walked, placing one trembling foot ahead of the other, often blundering into trees and brambles in the growing darkness, sometimes falling and then somehow pulling myself up again, I knew only that, whatever happened to me as a result of the terrible thing I had done, I was glad.

Since I had heard the school bus continue on past the hunters' blind, I knew that my precious Nicholas had been safely delivered to the arms of his loving parents.

Nothing else mattered to me.

The long yellow finger of the Cape Fear light was sweeping across the point as I finally stumbled to the edge of the pine forest and stood gazing down at my home. Confirming my worst fears, uniformed men stood before the cottage, and there were several vehicles pulled up in the drive, including the blue and white sheriff's car and a muddy green station wagon with an official emblem painted on its side.

Before I could assign meaning to the sight before me, or even think of fleeing, a dazzling beam of harsh white light lanced out from the side of one of the vehicles, and I heard a stranger's voice shouting, "There he is! The dog's up there in the trees!"

Too weary to run, too frightened even to slink back into the shelter of the pine forest, I remained standing shakily where I was, blinking myopically in the blinding glare of the spotlight, as shadowy figures ran up the slight hill toward me.

"Meteor! Meteor, boy, where have you been?"

Then, suddenly, my Nicholas was there beside me, his small face streaked with tears, his little arms clutched with painful tightness around my neck. "Oh Dad, he's been hurt," wailed the boy, as though his own heart were breaking. "Meteor's hurt!"

And then Robert was there too, lifting me up in his strong, gentle arms, leaning close to examine the wound in my head, whispering soft words of encouragement. "Take it easy old fellow. You just relax now, and we'll get you home."

Home. Never had a single word carried with it such a weight of feeling and emotion. Home. That was all I could think of, all I wished for . . . to be home.

Bewildered, trusting in my good master, I allowed myself to be carried down to the cottage, past the waiting strangers who I was sure had come to take me away. But instead of stepping forward, the men stood back to let us pass. Their stern features softened with concern as we mounted the stoop and I imagined I saw a tear sparkling in the corner of one man's eye.

Laura, her lovely features strained with worry, was waiting for us at the door, my favorite old blanket folded across her arms. "Gently," she ordered Robert, then leaned to kiss the matted fur of my snout. "Be very gentle with him, dear."

The remainder of the evening unfolded like a slow, hazy dream. The policemen and a game warden wearing a pointed hat stood by the door. They remained there for a long time, speaking in low tones with Robert, while Nicholas and Laura fussed over me by the fire, cleaning the worst of the grime from my tangled coat with warm, damp cloths and pouring delicious hot broth into me.

Not caring what else happened as long as my family had forgiven me, I lay there in my favorite spot, letting the blessed heat radiate into my half-frozen bones and whimpering only whenever something hurt far too much for silence.

In due time, the officials went away, having filled out their many reports, and promised Robert they would call to let him know if he was needed further. Though it strained me to breathe, I remained quite still by the fire, happy just to be home again and surrounded by those I loved.

It was very late by the time Doc Carlsen, the stoop-shouldered old vet who had been giving me my annual shots since I was a pup, arrived, apologizing and red-eyed from having been out delivering a troublesome foal somewhere far out in the county.

Doc carefully looked me over, peering down

over the tops of his odd half-spectacles and discovering with his strong but gentle fingers several new places that I had not even realized hurt.

"Well," he finally said as he deftly slipped a needle into a thick fold of skin at the back of my neck and stroked my fur, "he's had a pretty rough go of it, but I think he'll be no worse for the wear in a week or two. I've just given him something to put him to sleep while I stitch him up here and there."

There was another tiny bee sting of pain beside the spot where the first needle had gone in. "And that's an antibiotic," said Doc, "to prevent infection."

I felt the world slipping away as the old vet beamed down over the tops of his specs at me. "Damned fine animal you've got here," I heard him saying to someone in the room as my eyelids slid shut of their own accord. "Whoever would have ever thought it of this one?"

In fact, I limped around the cottage for more than the predicted two weeks after that memorable night, and every aching joint and bruised muscle in my body reminded me hourly of my ordeal in the wetlands. During the time that I was healing, I learned that the hunters—two factory workers from faraway Charleston—had indeed been quite drunk and lost to boot, when they had fired their guns at me in the wildlife preserve.

Still, the drunken hunters might have gotten clean away, had they not in their stupidity gone back to their truck and then driven straight to the sheriff's office in Thunderbolt to complain about the "mad" dog that had been shot at and escaped into the marsh after he attacked them without provocation.

Unfortunately for the men, Nicholas' school bus driver had already arrived at the same sheriff's office to report that he had heard gunfire dangerously close to the public road he drove twice daily. Of course, the local game warden had been immediately called. And, with the abashed hunters sobering up in a jail cell, the lawmen had driven out to the island to investigate.

Since I had failed to return home, more lawmen had been called, and they were in the process of initiating a search for me when I had staggered out of the pine forest.

I was not yet out of my bandages when the weekly *Coastal Reporter* ran a large photo of me with Nicholas kneeling proudly at my side. In a long and overly dramatic story that Robert insisted on reading aloud to everyone, I was proclaimed a canine hero.

Though I felt that I did not really deserve quite so much fuss and honor for doing no more than any loyal dog would have done for his family, late that night as I lay on my blanket at the foot of my precious boy's bed, I could not help but wonder if dour old Sam Wilson, the champion breeder who had once declared me useless, had chanced to see my picture in the newspaper.

Chapter 13

DANGER

By his ninth year, Nicholas had become a fairly accomplished naturalist and outdoorsman. A slender, wind-burned lad who ran like the wind and knew the secret habits and habitats of most of Cape Fear's varied wildlife, he already knew many of the Latin names of the birds and animals that dwelt on our remote island and most of those living in the sea around it.

Quiet and soft-spoken like his father, Nicholas was an obedient boy who respected his parents' judgment in almost all things. Lately, he had, by being always careful and punctual, earned the right to prowl the dunes, the forest and the surrounding salt marshes on his own, in pursuit of his beloved nature studies. There was only one condition.

I was that condition.

Nicholas was allowed to explore the beach, the forest and the edges of the great salt marsh—a place that was home to many creatures that were as dangerous as they were beautiful—only when accompanied by me.

"Meteor must always go out with you," Robert had told him on the day they had discussed the terms of the boy's freedom, "to keep you out of trouble."

"But Dad," Nicholas had protested, casting a guilty sidelong glance my way, "dumb old Meteor's always frightening off my birds whenever he thinks he smells a stupid rabbit. And last week he trampled right over a clutch of turtle eggs that I was going to take to school."

I closed my eyes and pretended to doze, shocked by the ungrateful boy's casual betrayal of one who had devoted a lifetime to his care but smugly certain of what his father's answer would be.

"Well, I'm afraid you'll just have to put up with him if you want to roam the island by yourself," was Robert's predicted reply. "When Meteor is with you, your mother and I don't worry," he explained, "because we know that he'll never let anything bad happen to you."

If dogs could smile, my grin that day would have stretched from ear to ear. Nicholas grumbled a bit, but, of course, he accepted his father's condition.

Thereafter, the lad and I trekked off together almost every Saturday in pursuit of rumored dens of foxes, a rarely seen variety of crane, collections of seashells, snakes' eggs, burrowing moles, crawfish. . . . The list was endless.

Always, I was right by his side, doing my best to stay out of his way and constantly suppressing my own desire to go tearing off in pursuit of the many fascinating scent trails we encountered along the way.

❦

It had been nearly a year later when we set out one bright May morning in Nicholas' ninth year, to examine the starfish in the tidal pools on a rocky stretch of beach beyond the lighthouse.

The boy had been at it for almost an hour, crouched over a large pool of surging seawater, lifting and examining one barely mobile starfish after another, while he patiently waited for the outgoing tide to recede fully so that he could climb into the water and wade around with the starfish.

Bored with the dull activity, I lay atop a large black rock, warming myself in the spring sunshine, while I was keeping one wary eye on him.

Both of our heads suddenly popped up, as a strange gasping moan sounded nearby.

I got to my feet, sniffing the air for signs of danger and scanning the surrounding terrain for the source of the odd noise. Then we both heard it again: a low, anguished sound of labored breathing.

It seemed to be coming from behind a tall weathered outcropping of stone that jutted out into the sea just beyond the tidal pools. I trotted toward the outcropping to investigate, but Nicholas ran past me and started scaling the steep, slippery stones.

Barking a stern warning to wait, I hurried after him. But he went on climbing higher and higher, heedless of my cries.

I began climbing the steep rocks myself, but I found that my paws were ill-suited to gaining traction on the slick, seaweed-slimed surface.

Nicholas, on the other hand, went up and up effortlessly; the thick rubberized treads of his dirty white tennis shoes provided an excellent grip on the sheer sides of the stone.

Before I could stop him, he disappeared over the summit and was gone.

Still barking frantically, I detoured around the large outcropping and came upon a narrow strip of beach, beyond which the sea bottom was known to drop off abruptly into hidden holes of unknown depth. Nicholas was sitting on the sand, hurriedly peeling off his shoes and blue jeans in preparation for entering the cold, dark water.

Sick with worry, I raced down to the boy and practically bowled him over in my eagerness to get between him and the dangerous shore. Nicholas looked at me as if I had gone mad. Then he set his jaw in determination and advanced toward the water. "Get out of the way, Meteor," he ordered.

I growled and held my ground.

"You dumb dog!" he shouted angrily. "We've got to save him."

I cocked my head in puzzlement. What was the boy talking about? As far as I could determine, he was the only one who needed saving from his own folly.

A loud, pain-wracked groan exploded almost

at my back, which caused me to spin around and stare.

There, nearly submerged in the dark, roiling water, its head resting on the narrow shelf of shoreline, lay a great black monster, its heaving sides slicked with blood that spewed in a cloud of pink spray from the breathing hole on the top of its head.

"It's a baby whale!" Nicholas shouted, striding past me and plunging waist deep into the water to stand beside the terrifed creature's head. It opened its gaping mouth, revealing a row of glistening teeth, each the size of a large salt shaker, and gazed at me with a huge brown eye.

"There now, take it easy, boy," whispered Nicholas to the whale, which did not look like a *baby* anything to me. He patted the thing's gigantic brow and scooped a handful of the bloody froth from around the breathing hole.

"I've read about this," he told the distressed whale, as he peered closely at the awful stuff in his hand. "You've got an infection that's been spread among Atlantic whales, and you're feeling very sick and a little dizzy right now.

"It'll get better by itself," he concluded, "but you can't stay here on the shore." Then he patted the whale's head again and pointed to the open sea. "You've got to get back out into deep water before the tide goes out all the way and leaves you stranded."

To my horror, Nicholas moved deeper into the water and began tugging at one of the great creature's submerged limbs, trying to coax it away from the shore. The frightened whale squealed pitifully. Then it rolled its eye seaward, and I followed its panicked gaze and saw what it was trying to see.

An icy hand of terror gripped my heart as I spied three large triangular fins knifing through the water not a stone's throw from where Nicholas stood immersed to his chest.

Sharks!

Attracted by the blood scent and the distressed cries of the juvenile whale, they had come to feed.

And Nicholas, my darling boy, the shining light of Robert and Laura's lives, was helpless in the water between them and their meal.

Never have I reacted so quickly or fearlessly as I did in that moment. Plunging into the cold water, I paddled to the boy's side and gripped the tail of his shirt in my jaws.

Nicholas turned in annoyance, raising a hand to push me away. And then he saw the approaching marauders. His eyes widened in fear. He stared at the approaching killers as though hypnotized, and then he slowly struggled toward the shore.

Too late, I remember thinking.

It was far too late for either of us to escape those pitiless flashing teeth. Nicholas and I would simply disappear into the sea without a trace. And Laura and Robert would spend the rest of their lives mourning, never even knowing what had become of us.

Unwilling to surrender us to such a bloody and anonymous fate, I yanked viciously on the boy's shirt, snapping him out of his trance. He began to swim strongly as the lead predator, a deadly sand tiger shark not less than twelve feet in length, rolled over and spread its huge jaws to attack.

And then a miracle occurred!

An immense boil of water rose up beneath the attacking shark. Something rose from the seabed, striking it squarely in the belly. The shark was flung high into the air, its back broken from the force of the impact.

All about us the water began to seethe and churn and fill with blood as some mighty unseen savior from the ocean depths dispatched the brutal killers one after another.

Nicholas and I dragged ourselves gasping from the water and lay on the warm sand, grateful to have escaped with our lives. Then we heard a squeal from the baby whale and looked up to see it being gently nudged away from the shallow shoreline by a gigantic barnacled creature that I could only assume was its mother.

The huge sea creature that had just saved our lives turned a soft, intelligent eye our way and looked at us for the briefest of moments. Then it turned majestically and guided its precious charge out toward the safety of the open sea.

For many minutes, Nicholas and I lay unmoving on the sand as our heartbeats slowly returned to normal. Then the boy grasped the thick hair at the back of my neck and thanked me for saving him, though we both knew full well that my puny effort had been nothing more than a futile gesture of my loyalty and love for him. At least, I thought, as I watched him pulling his jeans up over his still trembling legs, the boy had learned something of value today.

"Now," Nicholas said, getting to his feet and

examining the ripped tail of his wet shirt, "the question is how we're going to explain this to Mom."

It is, as I may have already mentioned, a great pity that the Maker did not in His wisdom see fit to endow dogs with the power of speech. I would have enjoyed pointing out to young Nicholas that he was every bit as noble and as foolhardy as his father for having so thoughtlessly risked his life for another.

But my pride in the boy was tempered by my fear for where such selfless instincts might lead him in the future.

After that incident, I never again took for granted the happiness that our little family had enjoyed for so long. And, from that time on, I never stopped looking for the subtle warnings of approaching danger.

Chapter 14

CHRISTMAS

Marking as it did the birth of the Savior and of our Nicholas, not to mention my arrival and the union of the two people who created our world, Christmas at Sea Pines Cottage had always been the happiest and most wonderful of times imaginable, even in the days when Robert and Laura had little but their love for one another and the boy to sustain them through the harsh Cape Fear winters.

By the time of the thirteenth Christmas after Nicholas' birth, the family had become truly prosperous.

Never before had so many glittering symbols of the joyous season been evident at Sea Pines Cottage. Inside and out, the cottage was fairly aglow with colored lights. The sounds of laughter and stereo recordings of softly singing choirs echoed through every room, and the scents of freshly cut greenery and the baking of cookies filled with spices made even sniffing the air an exercise in sensory delight.

For weeks before the great day, a delicious aura

of intrigue had surrounded the annual Christmas preparations, as Robert and Laura crept about like spies, smuggling strangely wrapped parcels back and forth between shed and cottage in the middle of the night.

Nicholas, too, was caught up in the wave of secrecy, often locking himself in his room to carve and paint and bang away for hours on the secret projects that he intended as gifts for his parents.

Oh, it was a wonderful time.

I was perhaps a bit past my prime by then, in canine terms at least. But though it sometimes pained me just a bit to raise myself from my favorite old tattered blanket in the chilly mornings, my health was still robust enough that no marauding raccoon or fox dared cross the boundaries I had marked around the cottage. There were many surprised rabbits who still barely managed to escape my wild pursuits through the pines.

On Christmas Eve, it had become a tradition at Sea Pines Cottage for the family to gather before the blackened fireplace in the old main room for Nicholas' birthday. This was done out of respect for the Savior, whose own birth was celebrated on the following day, but also so that Nicholas' special day would not be lost in the rush of Christmas festivities.

It had also become traditional over the years for the family to exchange their most personal gifts at the Christmas Eve gathering.

All day it had been snowing. It covered the pine forest with a soft white mantle and filled the old cottage with the magical sparkle of a fairy-tale castle.

Red-cheeked from last minute errands in the snow, Robert and Nicholas stamped into the main room and settled themselves in the comfortable furniture before the hearth. I had just taken my place by the woodbox, when Laura, radiant in a long, flowing robe of red satin, entered from the new part of the house and placed a tray containing a small cake with candles burning on it beside a pot of steaming chocolate on a low table.

"Now," said Robert, when everyone had a mug of chocolate in their hands, "we are gathered here to celebrate the thirteenth birthday of Nicholas. Happy birthday, son!"

Then Robert and Laura began to sing slightly off-key, while Nicholas managed to look both embarrassed and pleased. When his parents had finished their song, he blew out the candles with a single breath.

"Speech!" called Laura, as she did every year. "No presents until we have a speech."

Nicholas blushed, then he stood before the fire and looked into the faces of his parents. As he stood there, tall and handsome in the glowing firelight, I suddenly realized that the boy I had loved and cared for was on the brink of manhood, and I choked back a sigh of regret. For in the coming year, the child would be leaving us to attend a boarding school on the mainland, and all our lives would be changed once again. And, when he returned from the faraway school, I knew my Nicholas would no longer need this foolish old dog to look after him.

But that night we were having a celebration. So I put away my sadness and concentrated on the boy as he formed his thoughts before speaking to his parents.

"Mom," he finally said, raising his mug in tribute, "and Dad, I just want to thank you both for letting me grow up here in the forest by the sea, and for giving me a life that any boy would be grateful to have."

His adolescent voice suddenly cracked and I saw a tear streak his soft cheek. "I'll be going away to school next year," he continued, "away from you and Meteor and the forest and the sea and everything else that I love. . . . But I want you both to know that my heart will always be here in this house, in this room, where I have always felt warm and safe and protected."

Robert and Laura sat staring in stunned silence at their handsome son, for never before had Nicholas made such a profound declaration of his feelings. And previous birthday speeches had always been comic monologues filled with joking references to presents or to some mischief the boy had gotten into during the previous year.

Laura emitted a small sob. Then, suddenly, she and Robert were both standing and reaching for Nicholas. In her eagerness to reach the boy, Laura stumbled against the low table and Robert caught her in his arms, just as he had that day outside the cottage so many years before.

Robert kissed her flushed, lovely face and laughed as they gathered their son to them, hugging him tightly and vowing that they would always be there for him, and assuring him that he did not have to go away to boarding school, if he did not wish to.

Nicholas, with far more maturity than is common for a lad of his tender years, kissed them both, reminding them that his dream of someday becoming a marine biologist depended upon his getting the best possible grounding in science and math courses that were simply not available at the tiny rural high school in Thunderbolt.

When their emotions had finally settled, the loving family sat and ate the birthday cake and exchanged their gifts, which were, again by long tradition, all things they had made for one another with their own hands.

After the wrapping paper had been picked up and all the thanks and compliments were done, Nicholas got up and slowly walked around the room, extinguishing all of the lights.

Finally, there was no illumination in the room but the flickering firelight from the hearth and the twinkling glow of Christmas lights through the two mullioned windows by the old front door.

Then Nicholas returned and squeezed his lanky adolescent body in between Robert and Laura on the old sofa. For the next hour, the three of them held their arms around one another and sang lovely Christmas carols before the fire, which was the last and most beautiful of the family traditions they celebrated on Nicholas' birthday every year.

I lay silently in my place by the woodbox, listening to their voices raised in song. As the clean white snowflakes continued to drift past the windows from heaven above, I solemnly thanked the Maker for all that we had been given and prayed that He would always protect my little family from harm.

But always is a human word that has no meaning in the vast world of God and nature.

And the harm that I long had feared might befall my little family was already with us in that snug, firelit room that Christmas Eve, though none of us had yet recognized it for what it was.

Chapter 15

HARM

The first sign that something was terribly wrong came the very next day.

We had spent a wonderful Christmas morning together, as we opened presents before the gorgeous tree in the high-ceilinged family room of the new wing, and later tramped out into the cold to watch Nicholas sliding down a snow-covered dune on a round metal saucer that Robert had fashioned from the lid of a trash can.

Somehow the expedition out to the dunes to enjoy the novelty of seeing the results of a heavy snowfall beside the sea ended with everyone flinging balls of the frozen stuff at one another, while I jumped and yelped and ran frantically about in pursuit of errant snowballs.

By the time we returned to the cottage for our Christmas dinner, everyone was laughing and pleasantly exhausted from the unaccustomed activity. Laura left "her men" to stoke the fire while she attended to the meal. As she stepped into the kitchen, she stopped suddenly and put her hand to the wall as if steadying herself.

"Laura!"

"Mom!"

Robert went immediately to her and asked, "What is it?"

She raised her hand dismissively, saying, "Nothing. Just a silly ringing in my ears. I'm sure it's just the air pressure; there's a storm coming." Shaking her head, she added, "I'm fine."

Glancing up at the mistletoe, she reached up and kissed Robert and then went singing into the kitchen. The three of us looked at each other. Worry that it might be something serious was pushed aside as Laura called for help with serving.

Silver and china and sparkling crystal gleamed on the holiday table in the spacious dining room as Nicholas carried in a bowl of steaming vegetables and Robert lit the candles and poured the wine.

When all was in readiness, father and son stood dutifully by their chairs, waiting for Laura to bring the turkey, which she had been fussing over in the new modern kitchen.

When after a few minutes his mother did not appear, Nicholas impatiently called her name. He and Robert looked at one another, and fear replaced the concern when she did not immediately reply, and a small frown of worry creased Robert's brow.

He was just about to go to see what had become of her, when the kitchen door swung open and Laura appeared, her face slightly flushed, and her eyes sparkling with uncharacteristic brightness. She stood there shakily balancing the heavy platter in her hands. Robert rushed forward to help her, but before he could reach the doorway, the tray clattered to the floor, flinging the turkey and mounds of dressing across the polished floor boards. Then Laura's knees slowly gave way beneath her, and she collapsed.

For the first time since they had been together, Robert was not able to prevent her from falling.

We all rushed to Laura's side and Robert lifted her gently in his strong arms. "Oh what a mess I've made," she whispered, looking at the scattered ruin of the beautiful Christmas dinner.

"Son, call the doctor," ordered Robert, cradling Laura like a fragile doll.

"No!" said Laura, looking pleadingly into Robert's worried eyes. "It's nothing," she said. "I just got a little dizzy from the heat in the kitchen and all the activity this afternoon. Put me down on the sofa and I'll be fine in a minute. Honey," she told Nicholas, "try to save the turkey before Meteor gets into it."

But the turkey was the last thing on my mind. Something was very seriously wrong, and I could think of no way to protect her from it. I watched as Robert reluctantly carried her to a sofa before a tall window in the adjoining family room, while Nicholas got onto his knees and attempted to salvage the turkey.

"I still think I should call the doctor," Robert fussed, placing a hand on Laura's forehead. "You feel hot."

"Of course I'm hot! I've been in the kitchen.

I'm perfectly all right," Laura insisted. She craned her neck to look over the back of the sofa at Nicholas, who had replaced the turkey on its tray and lifted it to show her that it was fine. "The turkey is saved," she laughed. "I feel like such an idiot. I don't know what came over me."

"You could be coming down with something," Robert muttered suspiciously.

"Don't be silly," said Laura, pushing him away and getting to her feet. "You know me. I never get sick. Now let's go and eat our dinner before everything is cold."

Robert grudgingly allowed her to return to the table. And for the rest of the day, she did, indeed, seem to be perfectly fine, laughing and eating and joking about the secret ingredient she had added that made the turkey so delicious. It was, she confided after a sip of wine, just a hint of floor wax.

After a while, Robert and Nicholas finally relaxed, convinced that the disturbing incident was the result of overexertion and excitement on Laura's part.

That Christmas Day turned out to be one of the happiest and most memorable we had ever shared.

But Laura was not perfectly fine at all.

For though the progress of the insidious disease that had first shown itself when she had stumbled on Christmas Eve was agonizingly slow, throughout the winter there were more little accidents and unexplained dizzy spells.

Robert and Nicholas were not always present when Laura was temporarily seized by the progressively worsening spells. On those occasions when they were present, she always managed to convince them, and herself, that whatever had happened was simply the result of clumsiness or tiredness.

I was not so easily deceived, however, and I began to spend more and more of my time with Laura, the one family member who had never before needed my help. She had always been the strongest and most capable of my three humans.

Spring came, and then another summer appeared.

With the arrival of warmer weather, Laura's spells became fewer in number, and they were far milder when they did occur. Sometimes the attacks lasted only a moment and consisted of nothing more serious than her need to steady herself as she worked at her potter's wheel.

I dared to allow myself to hope that Laura's strong and healthy body was at last fighting off the disease, the way that colds and infections are often fought and overcome without medicine. But deep in my heart I think I knew that Laura's condition was not really going to go away, and I guarded her more closely than before.

There was nothing else that I could do.

The first crisp days of autumn came again, and Nicholas finally went away to school, leaving a great void in all our lives.

The boy hugged my neck and bade me look after his parents while he was away. And my heart ached at the emotion in his voice when he took his leave of me.

Robert and Laura smiled bravely as they packed

his clothes and belongings into the Jeep. But that night, when they returned alone from the school a hundred miles away, they clung to one another on the old sofa before the fireplace, and both their cheeks were wet with tears.

Outside the silent cottage that now seemed so empty, a cold wind whistled through the tops of the pines. Dozing off in my warm spot beside the woodbox, I dreamed for the first time not of rabbits, but of romping down a sunlit beach with Nicholas when he was small. And I suddenly longed for the feel of his tiny fingers tugging roughly at my ears and tried to recall exactly the sound of his high-pitched child's laughter.

However, everything had changed once more.

Chapter 16

CHANGES

Another autumn came.

Then, one frigid morning in late November, as I trotted importantly about the property, marking old boundaries and sniffing the cold salt air for traces of the approaching storm that was promised by the low, dark clouds scudding over the sea, I heard a deafening crash.

My old heart lurched in fear as I ran around to the shed and noticed the door to Laura's studio was half open.

I found her inside, lying on the floor beside the toppled wreck of her beloved potter's wheel.

"Faithful old Meteor," she said, reaching out with trembling fingers to touch my paw. "I should have known that you would be the one to come running. Please find Robert, if you can."

Her sea-green eyes surveyed the broken wheel and the mess of crumbled clay, and she smiled ruefully. "I seem to have had another little accident."

Never have I run so fast or barked so urgently. I

found Robert in the main room, reviewing the pages of a newly completed manuscript, and fairly dragged him outside to the shed.

What happened after that is slightly dim in my memory. After Robert had gotten her into the house, there was a great deal of confusion and telephoning. And then I heard a familiar sound from many years ago as the great clattering bulk of a white Coast Guard rescue helicopter settled onto the drive before the cottage.

The old oak door opened, and Robert stepped outside, as he carried our Laura bundled up in a swaddle of blankets once again.

My entire life passed before my eyes as I watched him walk slowly to the roaring machine and place her inside. Then a crewman helped him in, and the door was closed.

The helicopter rose up toward the dark clouds and flew away, just skimming the tops of the timeless dunes.

I watched until it was no more than a tiny speck on the storm-darkened horizon. Then I went into the cottage and settled in my favorite spot beside the woodbox to pray.

When Robert brought Laura home from the hospital, she seemed to be as good as new. But Robert now wore a perpetual frown of worry on his square, handsome face. He was reluctant to leave her alone, even for a moment. They spent many hours talking about things of which I had no knowledge: tests, something about bears, operations and a knife.

All of it reminded me of the only test with which I was familiar, and I had failed it miserably. Had she failed such a test, too? Unable to understand any of it, I had no idea if Laura was going to be all right.

Of course, Laura claimed all was well, and she would be fine, but Robert could not make the concern and fear leave his soulful eyes.

The doctors had declared that Laura had a brain tumor, one that caused her to lose her balance and make her hands shake. And if the tumor wasn't removed, it would continue to grow and cause permanent damage that would make our lovely, strong Laura unable to walk, make pottery or even smile.

All the whispering and discussions were about the treatments suggested by the doctors, most of which could cause the same damage to her as the tumor itself. After untold hours of going over the same things, Laura finally insisted that they stop talking about it until after the new year and Nicholas had returned to school. She was having a "good" period that hopefully would last through the holidays, so she forbade Robert to worry the boy with the details of her illness, until they had decided what they were going to do.

Changes are hard for an old dog, and the changes that year seemed almost unbearable. Nicholas left home; Laura got sick. Nothing was the same.

Nicholas' first visit home from school was a week before Christmas, and he found the house devoid of any of the seasonal decorations for which we had all become accustomed. His father told him that they were going to start a new tradition of waiting to decorate until he came home, so they could do it together. The boy was skeptical of the explanation, particularly since his father said it very seriously and with only a semblance of a smile.

Of course, the real reason was that Robert had not allowed Laura to do any of it, for fear she would fall off a ladder or worse. He had been unable to motivate himself to do it alone, in spite of his wife's wanting everything to be as normal as possible for their son. Finally, she insisted, and he grudgingly gathered all the decorations to await Nicholas' return.

After explaining to Nicholas that his mother had fallen off a chair in her studio and the doctor recommended that she stay off her feet as much as possible, Nicholas was put in charge of gathering the greenery.

It was one part of the "new tradition" that I thoroughly enjoyed. Nicholas and I went out into the pine forest to gather the boughs and branches that had become an important part of the family Christmas traditions. We seldom spent time together, just the two of us, anymore.

In spite of their attempts to keep her illness a secret, Nicholas seemed intuitively to know that all was not well, and he spent the entire holiday close to his mother, constantly leaping up to fetch things for her and sitting by her feet before the fire for long hours to tell her every detail about his school.

He was sure to always be in the house when it was time to prepare meals, so he could be there to help. He watched his mother lean heavily on his father's arm as they climbed the stairs to their hideaway bedroom, the room where he'd been born.

He cried the last night he was home. He had tried to get his father to talk about it, but it was to no avail, and his mother insisted all was well, or would be.

While the house had looked as it always did at Christmas, it felt different. Laura's not participating in everything, Robert's continual worry and Nicholas' fear kept the festivities at a minimum.

Finally, the morning of Nick's departure was at hand, and everyone cried, making no attempt to hide the emotions that they had been keeping inside. He knelt down and hugged my neck and whispered in my ear to watch over his mother and protect her the way I had always protected him. If dogs could cry, I certainly would have done so at that moment.

Robert took Laura back into the house, and I stood watching as the taxi took my boy away. The lump in my throat stayed for many minutes.

A few weeks later, Robert took me for a run on the beach, while the cold wind swirled the sand around us as the whitecapped waves crashed on shore. My old joints were getting creaky, so we didn't really do much more than walk, except for a short game of fetch. When I limped toward him depositing yet another piece of driftwood at his feet, he sat down on the sand, and I sat next to him, panting to regain my composure.

We looked out at the sea, and he put his arm around my shoulders.

"Cat's-paws," he said.

Cat's-paws on the surface of the ocean are caused by the wind making little ripples that look like a cat had been walking there, but they mean that an existing calm will soon be over.

Entwining his fingers in the ruff of my neck, he told me that he and Laura were going to Atlanta so she could have the tumor in her brain removed with something he called a Gamma Knife. I shuddered in fear at the sound of it. A knife, her brain, what kind of monstrous thing were they going to do to her?

Robert seemed to sense my revulsion and petted me.

"It's okay, boy. It will make her all better. It's a special knife that is really a kind of light that goes directly to the tumor and burns it away. Of course, we won't know how successful it will be for months, but it could make her all better."

I licked Robert's face and tasted salty tears. I knew then that he wasn't at all sure she would get better, that what they were going to do would make her our old Laura again. I rested my chin on his shoulder as we watched a dark line of clouds on the horizon proving the cat's-paws right. There would be an end to the calm we had had all Christmas season.

As we walked back to the house, not wanting to stay away any longer in case Laura needed something, Robert said that while they were in Atlanta, I would be going to Sam Wilson's place and that he hoped I didn't mind too much.

I barked my acceptance and jumped up as best I could for my old bones, wanting Robert to know that I would do anything if it helped make Laura well again.

"Of course, when we get back, I'm going to count on you to help keep her safe."

⁂

A few days later, I was back at Prairiewood Kennels biding my time until I could go home, praying with every fiber of my being that Laura would be all right.

One afternoon I lay in a small patch of winter sun. I looked up as footsteps approached my run. Not wanting to relinquish the healing warmth to my weary joints, I put my head on my paws again, assuming whoever it was would continue on. But the footsteps stopped at the gate of my enclosure, and a teenage boy stepped in, leaving several other boys his age outside.

"Hi, Meteor."

The voice was familiar but not instantly recognizable, as he knelt beside me and scratched my ears. I licked his hand in appreciation of the only attention or affection I'd been shown during my stay.

Continuing his gentle stroking, the young man told his friends that he played with me when I was a puppy, before his father had given me to the "strange dude at the lighthouse." I realized this was the small boy who visited me and my brothers and sisters every day after school years ago. But I also realized, with some consternation, that the "strange dude" he mentioned was my Robert.

Slowly I stood up, and so did he, and with his hand still resting on my head he said, "Remember the two poachers who shot up a school bus a few years ago?"

The boys outside the enclosure made comments like, "Yeah, boy were they lame," and "Can't get much stupider than that."

With pride in his voice, the teen told his friends that I was the dog who stopped the bad guys and got hurt in the process. He bent down and squeezed my neck.

"He's a real hero."

"Cool," said one of the other boys. "My dog would have turned tail and run."

"Well, not Meteor. He saved all the kids on the bus that day."

After rubbing my ears again, the boys left. As I watched them walk away playing air guitars, I stood a little taller, knowing that Sam Wilson was aware of the accolades I had received. He probably *had* seen my picture in the newspaper. Feeling proud, I could now look him in the eye. I wasn't the useless animal he had proclaimed me to be.

Laura's homecoming was a somber affair, with Robert lifting her from the car and placing her in a shiny new wheelchair. This was a chair she was to use until they were sure she wouldn't fall anymore.

One day when the winter weather was mild and only a couple weeks after her return, Robert and I took Laura outside and showed her our favorite old haunts.

We all pretended it was a great adventure, and Laura joked about feeling like a princess as she was being wheeled through the trees and down the steep path between the dunes. But even the bright winter sunshine and the pleasant sounds of nature could not dispel the chilly pall of fear that had settled over Sea Pines Cottage.

The remainder of winter was quiet for the three of us. Worry and fear kept Robert from his work, which made Laura concerned about him. Laura's hands still shook, so she was unable to make her pottery. In any case, they had yet to replace the potter's wheel that was broken in her fall. They were both miserable: her green eyes were no longer sparkling; his gray eyes were a little dimmer.

I watched, unable to do anything to help either of them. I felt helpless as I watched my little family seem to crumble before my weary old eyes, as the cold wind continued to howl around our house. The love was there, but the joy that had always filled our home seemed lost.

The one bright spot every day was when we three worked together. Robert and I helped Laura with her exercises. It was the only time when their smiles weren't forced or filled with sadness, and she was getting stronger. In time, she was able to use a walker instead of the wheelchair. And as winter was finally ending and the first green sprouts of spring flowers pushed through the softening soil, all she needed was a walking stick.

She was still weak and frail, not the strong and energetic Laura of days past, and I worried that she would never be the same. But she was with us and seemed to be getting better, and I thanked the Maker for that.

As spring approached, she was well enough that Robert felt he could leave her to my care and go to town for some needed supplies. I took the responsibility seriously, so when she said she wanted to go for a walk, I barked my disapproval. But she persisted, as she put on a parka and opened the front door. I tired to block the way by standing in the doorway, but she managed to slip around me and took a few steps outside.

"I'll be careful, Meteor. I don't want to go far, but I'm getting cabin fever, and Robert is too afraid to take me out, so I'm counting on you."

While I, too, was afraid for her, I was heartened by the stubbornness she was showing. She was getting stronger, and I hoped it meant that she was getting well. We hadn't been out. . . . She hadn't been out since our jaunt in the wheelchair, and while I didn't understand the words she said about cabin fever, I did understand her desire to be outside.

We moved slowly. I ignored the scent of field mice out to investigate the early spring sunshine. I never left her side, even when I spied a pair of rabbits who were in desperate need of chasing. I contained the urge to take off after them and continued on our little sojourn.

As we started to slow down because of the incline of the hill in front of us, I barked the suggestion that we return to the house by stopping and looking back, but Laura insisted.

"I just want to get to the top of the hill, so I can see the ocean. Then we'll go back. I promise."

I looked at her with some suspicion, but she seemed so happy to be out in the salty air—her cheeks pink for the first time in weeks—and she was breathing deeply, as a cool breeze rustled the foliage around us. There was a serenity I hadn't seen in her for many months, and she was looking more and more like our old Laura. With a false sense of well-being, I ran ahead to check out some of the delicious scents on the floor of the piney forest.

Her scream almost stopped my heart. I'd left her alone. How could I have been so stupid? How could I face Robert, if anything happened to her? I rushed to her side, instantly standing between her and the eastern diamondback rattlesnake that was coiled only a few feet away; its tail was making the hollow noise I'd come to recognize as fear. The snake was afraid of us and was simply protecting itself from what it thought was a threat.

Making sure Laura was behind me and I was far enough away so it couldn't strike out at me, I lowered my head and barked a warning at it— several, in fact. I lunged slightly and continued my incessant barking. Finally, it turned and slithered back into its den.

I immediately went to Laura and put my head under her free hand, and she took a deep breath. She was shaking, and I feared she might fall. Once again I looked at the house and barked, indicating in no uncertain terms that we needed to return to the safety of our home.

Rubbing my head, she said, "Thank you, Meteor. And you're right. We should go back now."

Inside the house, she thanked me again, hugging my neck and crying. "What would I do without you?"

We never mentioned our little escapade to Robert, as he would have been terrified of the incident. It was our secret. But when Laura suggested a few days later that Robert take her out, I helped convince him by pushing him toward the door and barking my approval of the plan.

Chapter 17

SPRING BREAK

As spring blossomed in full, it brought back to the pine forest the birds and wild creatures that we all so dearly loved. It allowed more trips out into the sunshine, trips that lasted longer and longer each time.

Robert tried to work but said he had problems concentrating. I knew it was his worry for Laura that stopped him, but he continued to try.

One of the supplies he had gotten the day of our rattlesnake incident was a new potter's wheel, and Laura was once again trying her hand at throwing. She was frustrated occasionally when her hands wouldn't do what she wanted, but she persevered.

Things seemed to be getting back to normal, or so I thought.

One warm, sunny afternoon while Robert was outside attending to some necessary task, I heard the sound of soft weeping from the sofa in the main room, where Laura had retired for her daily rest.

"Oh, Meteor," she whispered, when I walked up to her and silently nuzzled one of her small hands that still shook a bit.

She wiped her eyes and rubbed the spot on the back of my neck. "I'm sorry I let you see me crying," she said. "But I'm so worried about Robert."

Then I listened with a growing sense of wonder as Laura explained that she had always felt their meeting and coming together had been fated. She had given Robert the confidence he needed to succeed as a writer; he had encouraged her talent. She had taken care of him and nurtured his writing, his business and his damaged self-esteem—while he had made Sea Pines Cottage the wonderful home they all loved. They'd given each other Nicholas.

She murmured that the tumor might not be gone entirely or could grow again. She was worried that if that happened, Robert would be overly burdened by caring for her. What would happen to his writing if she were not there to push him through the rough patches? Who would handle his business? What would happen if all that were unfairly placed on his shoulders?

Laura paused, then she went on to express her confidence that Nicholas would grow up to be self-reliant and strong. He would survive, even if she were no longer around, for he had inherited those qualities of strength from her.

It was the first time either of them had mentioned the possibility of her death since she returned from the hospital. For some reason that was beyond my comprehension, today she desperately feared what would happen to Robert without her.

The love and concern in Laura's soft voice as she confided her innermost thoughts to me sent chills down my spine. Her courage and goodness seemed boundless. Never once as she spoke did Laura mention herself or the helpless sense of dread that she must be feeling, should these things come to pass.

"I think, Meteor," she said with sudden determination, "that I must do something positive. Nicholas will be coming home for spring break tomorrow, and I must do this thing for him and for Robert."

I confess that I really did not know what Laura meant when she said she had to do something. Only later would I remember and worry about those words. She was not much stronger than a pup, so I could not even begin to imagine what she *could* do. But then, I was so overwhelmed by the outpouring of love from her gentle heart that I admittedly attached no real importance to her talk of *doing something*.

For hers was the same selfless love that I had discovered early in our dear Robert. And, in my mind, simply being possessed of and keeping faith with such a magnificent and giving love as I had seen in Robert and Laura was all that any human could ever hope to do on this sad old earth.

I did not understand how the Maker could allow those two lovers ever to be separated and had faith that he would not.

Late that night, as they held one another close, I heard Laura asking Robert if he could launch the sailboat for her the next day. She would, she told him, like to cruise out onto the smooth green sea again and feel the warm breezes in her hair.

Robert seemed pleased by her request. He smiled and said that of course he would launch the boat. It would, he thought, make a fine surprise for young Nicholas when he returned home in the afternoon.

I lay in my old place in the bedroom window seat and watched the whirling beacon of the Cape Fear light as I listened to them talking. The hairs on my back stood up as I worried about how dangerous such an outing could turn out to be for Laura, if anything should happen to the frail boat.

After a while, Laura leaned closer to Robert and began to whisper softly.

Unable to hear any more, I made a solemn vow to keep an extra close watch over her when we went sailing on the morrow.

⁂

Early in the morning, Robert wheeled the little sailboat out into the bright spring sunshine and cleaned her decks and polished her brass. Then, with me barking encouragement at his side, he hooked her to the winch on the Jeep and slowly rolled the shipshape craft down the steep path to the beach.

After lunch, he stepped the varnished mast,

tightened the rigging and attached the sails. By midafternoon the boat was ready at last. Leaving it beached prettily on the sand at the water's edge, Robert returned to the cottage for Laura.

Looking as beautiful as she ever had in a striped sailing jersey and jeans, Laura waved and called out happily to me as Robert drove the Jeep down and parked beside the boat.

Leaning on Robert as she got out of the car and into the boat, she sat on a cushion in the cockpit. He then went around to the bow to loosen the line tethering the sloop to the shore.

I leaped joyfully onto the foredeck, thrilled by how healthy Laura appeared, and anticipated a brisk sail out beyond the cape. But Robert suddenly called out to me. I obediently jumped back onto the sand and ran to his side. "You stay here today, Meteor," he said. "Laura and I want to be alone."

My hearing is not as keen as it once was, and I was not sure that I had heard him correctly. So I jumped eagerly back into the boat. But Robert firmly took hold of me and put me back on shore. "No, Meteor," he gruffly commanded. "Go home and wait for Nicholas. I don't want him arriving to find an empty house."

Hurt and confused at being so suddenly excluded from the sailing party, I stood forlornly on the sand as Robert shoved the boat out into the surf and turned her into the wind.

I stayed there watching the little boat grow smaller and smaller against the rolling surface of the green Atlantic. When at last it disappeared behind the lighthouse, I turned and trotted back up the path to wait for Nicholas.

I waited for many hours on the front stoop of the cottage, as the shadows of the pines grew long with the coming of late afternoon. From time to time, I would get up and go to the top of the path between the dunes. From that vantage point, I anxiously scanned the empty sea for some sign of the sailboat and my beloved Robert and Laura.

But there was no sign.

Just before twilight, a rattling taxi came up the drive, and Nicholas climbed out. "Good old Meteor," he yelled. "How've you been boy?" I ran out to meet him, and he joyously threw his arms around me as the cab driver unloaded his luggage.

When the taxi had gone, Nicholas looked up in surprise at the silent cottage. "Where are the folks?" he asked.

With a sinking feeling in my stomach, I trotted to the top of the path, then turned back to bark at Nicholas. He frowned his father's frown and ran to join me. I cringed fearfully as he raised his eyes and peered out to sea.

"Well I'll be," he laughed. "Will you look at that!"

I followed his gaze down to the beach where Robert was just guiding the sailboat onto the sand. Nicholas whooped and took off running down the path, all gangly legs and arms.

I followed him as fast as I could, panting with the effort to catch up. Robert had just pulled the boat onto the beach and was looking up and hollering for Nicholas to come and help him.

Laura was sitting in the cockpit, smiling and waving.

By the time I reached the boat, father and son had it completely out of the water. Then, to my utter astonishment, Laura stood and allowed Nicholas to help her out. She hugged her son, then carefully walked the few steps to the Jeep without her cane or a strong arm. When she got into the front seat, I clambered in beside her and licked her face in a lavish show of relief and gratitude.

The sun sank slowly behind the dunes, and the beacon of the Cape Fear light began to revolve as we sat there watching Robert and Nicholas snug the sailboat down for the night.

"I told you I would do something," Laura proudly whispered, rubbing the spot on the back of my neck.

Looking into her beautiful sea-green eyes, I could see that she was tired, but very happy, too.

"Robert and I decided last night that we are going to fight this thing with every ounce of strength that we have," she declared. "We will not give in to it as long as the Lord gives us breath. We will fight it minute by minute and hour by hour, Meteor. But we will never give up. Our love and faith will get us through this dark time."

Robert and Nicholas were walking toward us, their arms linked around one another's waists like old comrades. The boy was listening solemnly as his father explained to him everything the doctors had told them. The surgery went well, but they wouldn't know for some time if it did what they hoped. Robert was telling him what

Laura had told me, that they would fight with every fiber of their beings and never give up.

Nicholas nodded and looked lovingly toward his mother.

Chapter 18

WAITING

Spring turned to summer, and Nicholas came home for his first extended stay. We wouldn't lose him again until September.

But September came too soon. The two and one-half months he was home flew by with romps in the ocean, picnics on the beach and sailing. We all sailed, almost every day. Sometimes it was before the picnic, sometimes it was after, but we sailed.

And as June slipped into July, Nicholas and I spent every morning foraging in our personal wilderness. I sniffed and chased, and he took pictures of everything from spider webs to whales.

On Independence Day, we four sat on the beach around a small bonfire, roasting hot dogs and marshmallows. These were all treats, since, as I had gotten older, Laura was concerned with my eating the right things to keep me healthy, which generally didn't include the best-tasting stuff like hot dogs and marshmallows. With my head in Nicholas' lap, we watched the fireworks from the mainland. I sighed in contentment. Laura and Robert kissed. It was like the old days.

As July became August, Laura seemed stronger, which made all of us happier. The summer even made me feel better, as my aged body moved more easily in the heat of the summer sun.

In spite of the good times and Laura's seeming improvement, there was still an uncertainty that colored everything we did. All of us were wondering if it would be the last summer, the last sailing trip, the last time we all would be together. But we pushed that uncertainty aside and enjoyed ourselves immensely, as though nothing in the world could touch us at Sea Pines Cottage.

But all good things must come to an end, and August seemed to rush to September and Nicholas left us. We were bereft of our young man and the joy he brought with him.

***

The autumn came with the dry pine needles carpeting the forest floor. Gold and red leaves covered the path to the dunes, and the wind howled in the tops of the trees.

Laura was her old self, back to throwing her pots and jars, having rid herself of the cane sometime in the middle of summer. Robert was writing once again, and life was returning to normal, with only occasional talk of the possible consequences of the brain tumor.

We stayed true to our pledge to fight the good fight and not give up.

Halloween filled the house with jack-o-lanterns and witches. Laura put a broomstick and cauldron on the front porch. Thanksgiving was a quiet affair with just the three of us—and turkey and pumpkin pie for me, a real treat.

The next day I woke up and saw Robert asleep, alone. Fear gripped my heart. Where was Laura? I got up from my window seat and padded downstairs, unable to run as I had in my youth.

I reached the living room limping slightly, and the sound of my nails clicking on the hardwood floor made Laura turn and look at me.

"Good morning, Meteor." She spread her arms and turned around. "What do you think?"

The house already smelled like Christmas, with a batch of gingerbread on the kitchen counter. The crèche was set up on the small gateleg table in the dining room. Stockings hung from the mantle; the animated Bob Cratchit and Tiny Tim were on the hearth next to my blanket. Laura was decorating for Christmas. I wondered what happened to the "new tradition" of waiting for Nicholas? This was better; it was the way it was supposed to be.

"Come on, we need to get the greenery. I want it done before Robert gets up."

She slipped on her parka, and we went outside. After I had done my business, we walked around, Laura pulling Nicholas' wagon, just as she did when he was a small boy. We loaded it with fragrant cuttings into which she twisted lights and hung them around the windows and filled the mantle, adding the pinecones we'd collected, as well as the shiny red apples she loved so much.

My heart raced when she climbed on to a chair and attached the beribboned mistletoe in the kitchen doorway. But she did it and got down without anything bad happening, and I was able to breathe a sigh of relief, as I heard Robert come down the stairs.

His eyes widened, and a smile spread across his face. He rushed to Laura and swept her into his arms and kissed her under the mistletoe. Christmas had come to Sea Pines Cottage.

One of my favorite traditions came after dinner that evening. Laura unwrapped the green candle holder she had made many years earlier and placed a simple white taper in it, set it on the window sill and lit it. Now strangers knew they were welcome.

It was only two weeks later that Nicholas came running through the door.

"I'm home," he hollered, tossing his duffle on the floor next to the door.

In the kitchen, Laura greeted him with hugs and kisses. I saw tears well from Nicholas' eyes. Robert came in and gave his son a strong manly handshake, then enveloped him in a bear hug. I was last to lavish attention and affection on our boy, and my licking finally came to an end when he jumped up.

"Enough, Meteor. You'll drown me." Their laughter filled the kitchen. We were together again. All of us.

A few days later, the family left for the day— Laura to the city for a special treat for Christmas dinner and the "boys," as Laura referred to Robert and Nicholas, had one last-minute gift to get. I stayed and guarded our home and hearth.

As twilight fell, Robert and Nicholas drove up but stopped at the old lightkeeper's cottage, and as I watched through the front window, encircled by the branches Laura and I had collected, the "boys" carried a cardboard box into the abandoned building. They stayed in there for a while, and I wondered what was keeping them. Just as I was about to give up my vigil, Laura's car pulled into the drive and up to the house.

I met her at the door, and there was something different about her as she swept into the house. Throwing her parka and purse on the floor, she knelt down and threw her arms around my neck. I felt the tears on my fur, and fear gripped my heart. Had something happened that would take her away from us? She said nothing but finally stood up and wiped the tears away. The lump returned to my throat.

Heaving a deep sigh, she picked up her things and put them away. Looking around she asked, "Where are the men folk?"

I ran to the window and barked. She followed. Together, we watched Robert and Nicholas exit the cottage and drive the remainder of the way up to the house.

Laura ran to the door and threw it open. I was not as fast, but I was at the door by the time they came in. She hugged both of them tightly, which brought back the lump in my throat. Robert held her at arm's length and worriedly asked, "What's wrong?"

"Nothing. I'm just happy to see you."

Unconvinced, Robert released her and turned to Nicholas, who had the same worried expression on his face. But her cheerfulness kept all of us from dwelling on the concern. She wanted to know what they had been doing in

the old cottage. They smiled and said it was a secret.

After a simple dinner, Nicholas took me outside for a walk. We wandered toward the lighthouse as the brilliant light skimmed the roof of
Sea Pines Cottage. Near the old lightkeeper's
place, Nick stopped and knelt next to me.

"I'm going to show you the present Dad and I
got Mom."

We went inside. Lighting a lantern, the boy
led me to the far corner of the main room. The
winter chill was being kept at a minimum by a
space heater. The cardboard box I'd seen Nick
and Robert carry into the building had been
placed in the corner, and curled inside, asleep,
was a puppy. Golden in the soft light of the
lantern, it reminded me of my sisters and brothers.

Nicholas knelt down and lifted it up into the
air, just as Robert had done to me so many seasons ago. It licked his face, as I had Robert's.

He set the animal down in front of me.

"What do you think, Meteor? Will Mom like
her?"

I sniffed suspiciously but found nothing un-
toward. She licked my nose, so I returned the
favor. Nicholas gathered her up and put one
arm around my neck.

"I'm counting on you to teach her how to
take care of Mom and watch over Sea Pines Cottage. I know it's getting pretty hard for you to
get around sometimes. Now she can do some of
the work for you."

Of course I knew that the Maker in his wisdom had given me more seasons than I had any

right to expect, and while I hoped for a few more, it was probably good to have young eyes watching things, young bones to chase and run. I wouldn't be here to watch over them forever. I nuzzled the pup again.

Nicholas put the puppy back in the box.

"We're going to give her to Mom tomorrow night. So you have to help keep it a secret until then."

The small creature curled herself up in the corner and slipped off to sleep again. I licked the top of her head and Nicholas patted mine. We looked at each other and then at the box. It was good.

Nicholas' birthday dawned bright and sunny, although the cold kept the fire in the fireplace going all day. The smell of cookies and cake filled the air. The Christmas tree twinkled in the corner, and it was surrounded by gifts of every conceivable size and shape. The candle on the windowsill was lit; the starlike lights sparkled in the greenery. It was magical. After the evening meal, the family gathered to celebrate Nicholas' fifteenth year.

As was always the tradition, Robert, Nicholas and I sat in front of the fire, waiting for Laura to appear. The moment arrived, and Laura came in wearing a new green and red plaid dress as she carried the cake, aflame with candles, and set it on the table in front of Nicholas.

His parents had given Nicholas a new camera and all the accessories needed to take underwater photographs. He was thrilled. He took pictures of all of us as we sat and admired our fine young man.

When it was time to exchange the personal Christmas gifts, things got decidedly untraditional. Laura announced that her special gifts would have to wait until tomorrow, because they wouldn't be ready until then. Robert and Nicholas looked quizzically at each other. What could they be?

Nicholas jumped up and said he needed to take me out for a walk. Laura questioned the need at that particular moment, but he looked at me for confirmation that I did indeed need to go out, and I obliged by getting down from my warm spot by the fire and barking my agreement.

We returned in only a few minutes with the wiggly puppy in Nicholas' arms, as she squirmed to get down. He rushed in and put the dog in his mother's arms.

"Merry Christmas, Mom."

"She's adorable." Laura lifted her and kissed her nose. As she set the small furry thing in her lap, she looked at me.

"Do you approve, Meteor?"

I barked and licked the puppy to show my approval. Laura gave me a radiant smile.

"What's her name?"

"We figured you'd want to name her."

"Guess I'll have to think about it." Laura got up and set the puppy next to me by the fire, and the creature crawled between my paws and rubbed her head on my muzzle, and then she curled up with a sigh. Rather than take my traditional spot on the window seat of the upstairs bedroom, I stayed downstairs to keep the youngster company.

During the night, I awoke to find the puppy gone. In my first cursory look around, I saw her at the window. She sat looking up into the night sky.

A sound came from my left, and I got up to investigate. I found Nicholas creeping down the stairs in his stocking feet. He rubbed my head as he stepped onto the cold wood floor of the main room.

"Hi, fella. I wanted a glass of milk." He glanced at the fireplace. "Where's the puppy?"

I yipped softly and looked toward the window. Nicholas laughed, "What's she doing?" Continuing to chuckle he went into the kitchen and returned carrying the desired milk and some of his mother's gingerbread cookies.

He poked the fire to try to get it to flame up again, and it did for a short time. It was long enough for him to finish his milk and cookies. Leaving the remnants of his snack on the coffee table, he rubbed my head and said good night. As he rounded the newel post, he looked over at the puppy again, who was still silently peering up into the dark.

"She's a stargazer, isn't she?"

The next morning the puppy was christened Star after Nicholas told his mother about the puppy's infatuation with the nighttime sky.

After breakfast, Nicholas, Star and I went out into the wilds of our little island home. I showed her where to find the fattest rabbits, the slowest squirrels and the snake dens to avoid. We went down to the beach and Nicholas threw a piece of driftwood for her to chase. Even in the cold, she ran into the surf to retrieve it and proudly brought it back and dropped it at Nicholas' feet.

I sat next to him wondering at the circle of life. Many moons earlier, I had been the pup running into the cold water, bringing my prize back to Robert. Now it was Robert's son and a new pup. I knew the Maker had given me a privileged life, and I was grateful for it. But I did regret knowing I probably wouldn't see Nicholas get much older, that this was likely my last Christmas. But the joy I had in living in this wondrous place with these incredible people had been a privilege.

The Cape Fear lighthouse light started its revolutions as darkness came to the island. Nicholas called to Star, and we three went back to the house where Nicholas dried the pup with an old towel and put her on the hearth near the fire to dry off. I smiled to myself, since dogs don't smile, when she walked around in circles before lying down, leaning against my blanket, but not on it.

The nap was refreshing for this old dog, and the pup was well rested, when Laura called our little family to dinner.

Once again, the table was set with china, silver and crystal. Lovely red and white flowers with greens, arranged in a vase that looked like a sleigh, was placed in the middle of the table. Robert stood at the head of the table, and Nicholas stood behind his own chair. Star and I sat near the wall, and she copied my every move. Laura called out that she was almost ready, to wait just one more minute.

Robert, Nicholas and I looked at each other

and held our breath. It was two years ago at this meal that Laura had had her first major episode and dropped the turkey. My heart raced, because I wanted her to be completely well. I remembered her tears when she came home only two days before. Were the tears for the knowledge that she wasn't getting better?

Robert had to keep himself from rushing to help her, and even Nicholas almost made a step forward as she entered the room carrying the roasted bird. We three sighed a collective breath of relief when she walked in unaided and set the platter on the table in front of Robert.

Forcing a smile, Robert picked up the carving knife and fork, but Laura spoke first.

"Just a minute," she said, gently laying her hand on his arm. "I have yet to give my gifts to you. The problem is, there's only one, so I'm afraid you are going to have to share it."

Robert and Nicholas looked at each other, as they wondered what sort of gift it could be.

"I've gotten the results of the latest tests, and it appears that they got the whole tumor and nothing is coming back. I'm cured."

The stunned silence gave her a chance to continue. "Of course, it isn't for absolute certainty for a couple of years, so I have to take the tests every six months. But it looks good, according to the doctor. I'll be fine."

I suddenly realized that the tears she shed the other day had been tears of joy, and my fears that she would leave us had been wrong. I heaved a sigh of relief.

"Oh, Mom. That's so great!" Nicholas said as he rushed and hugged her. Robert, tears streaming down his face, put down the fork and knife and held his wife as close and as tightly as he could without injuring her. He could find no words. Her laughter sounded like Christmas bells pealing.

I'd seen many a Christmas miracle in this house, but none compared with tonight. When the Maker finally calls me, I will be leaving my little family whole and in the goods paws of Star. I couldn't help but be overjoyed that they were all healthy and happy. Life was good.

Robert and Nicholas cleaned up the dinner things, and Laura made the hot chocolate, another tradition of the season.

As the three of them sat together on the couch, Star and I watched the Cape Fear light flash on the point, marking the passage of one minute and fifteen seconds of triumph for our little family.

It was one minute and fifteen seconds more that the Maker in His wisdom had granted us all, to live and love on this old earth.

It occurred to me then that no creature could ever ask for or expect more than that.

Star gazed out the window as she lay snug between my big front paws. We watched together as a brilliant meteor sped across the night sky.

I leaned my tired old head against her soft golden fur and sighed contentedly, telling her that this was Christmas at Sea Pines Cottage.

When New York artist Eliza Knight buys an old vanity table one lazy Sunday afternoon, she has no idea of its history. Tucked away behind the mirror are two letters. One is sealed; the other, dated May 1810, is addressed to "Dearest Jane" from "F. Darcy"—as in Fitzwilliam Darcy, the fictional hero of Jane Austen's *Pride and Prejudice*. Could one of literature's most compelling characters have been a real person? More intriguing still, scientific testing proves that the second, sealed letter was written by Jane herself.

Caught between the routine of her present life and these incredible discoveries from the past, Eliza decides to look deeper and is drawn to a majestic, two-hundred-year-old estate in Virginia's breathtaking Shenandoah Valley. There she meets the man who may hold the answer to this extraordinary puzzle. Now, as the real story of Fitzwilliam Darcy unfolds, Eliza finds her life has become a modern-day romance, one that perhaps only Jane herself could have written . . .

"Fascinating . . . pays tribute to Jane Austen's enduring ideals of romantic love."
Booklist

"O'Rourke's latest is mysterious yet romantic as she reveals secrets of Jane Austen's life."
Romantic Times

"This wonderfully conceived novel is fresh, original, and rewarding."
Susan Wiggs, *New York Times* bestselling author

Please turn the page for an exciting sneak peek at
THE MAN WHO LOVED JANE AUSTEN
coming next month in mass market!

Prologue

Chawton, Hampshire
12 May, 1810

The slender young woman hurrying along a lonely woodland path beyond the village of Chawton this night seemed heedless of the falling moisture that sprinkled her hair and dampened the shoulders of her light cloak.

It had rained in the afternoon, a hard spring shower that had passed over the wood in no more than ten minutes. And though the downpour hadn't lasted long enough to muddy the path that Jane now followed, the leaves of the overhanging trees were still shedding droplets that glittered like jewels in the cold moonlight.

As she moved through the silent wood Jane imagined the scandal that would erupt should a neighbor happen upon her in this lonely place. For she was a respectable young woman by any standard, the unmarried daughter of a clergyman with aristocratic family connections, and youngest sister to the owner of the great country house on which the village depended. Which circumstance rendered her midnight foray all the stranger. For Jane had never before dared nor even considered an adventure such as the one on which she was now embarked.

Yet here she was, gliding wraithlike through the dark forest, en route to a clandestine meeting with a man—a mysterious and possibly dangerous man—whom she had known for scarcely five days. She prayed that he would be at the appointed spot, as he had promised. And she felt her heart thundering in her breast at the mere thought of what she had committed to share with him this night. She who had long since abandoned all hope of ever finding love.

She was thirty-four years old—an unremarkable spinster who lived an unremarkable life in a house provided by her devoted brother and shared with her elder sister and their aged mother. And, until fewer than twenty-four hours ago, she had never known a lover's caress.

But last night that had changed. Now Jane wanted nothing more than to be again with the man. For he had reawakened her girlhood dreams of love and romance, all the lovely dreams she had so carefully preserved on countless sheets of neatly inscribed vellum that she kept hidden away in the deepest recesses of her closet.

Of course, she fully realized, going to meet him like this was madness. But then, she reminded herself, madness had been the hallmark of their brief but intense relationship, a relationship that had been doomed from the start. For she could not go with him and he could not stay.

And if they were found out, she knew to a certainty, scandal and disgrace would be her only reward.

But love knows not reason. And Jane did not care what consequences might ensue. For, in her mind, the risks she was taking to meet with her new-found lover tonight were as nothing compared to the dread she felt, of slipping into her old age without ever having tasted love.

❧

After a few more minutes she came to the edge of the woods, which bounded a broad meadow. Covered now in swirls of mist frosted by the light of a near-full moon, the grassy field had taken on an otherworldly look, like one of the fairy-tale landscapes she was forever imagining in her dreams. At the end of the path she hovered like a frightened deer, huddling in a pool of darkness beneath the dripping trees, until he should appear.

Presently, she heard the drumming of muffled hoofbeats from the far side of the meadow. Willing her joyously thudding heart to be still, Jane boldly detached herself from the sheltering shadows and advanced into the open, anxious not to waste a precious moment of the brief time they would have together.

Slowly a horseman emerged from the mist. Spying her moving through the grass, he altered the course of his great black steed to intercept her. Within seconds he reined to a halt beside her. His face was obscured beneath the brim of the tall hat he wore, and she ran forward to meet him as he dismounted. "I prayed you would come," she laughed, prepared to throw herself into his arms.

But instead of the joyous response she was anticipating, the rider nervously swept the tall hat from his head. The moonlight struck his plain, sun-reddened features and she saw to her mortification that he was not the one for whom she had so anxiously waited, but an awkward young servant named Simmons.

"Sorry, miss," the nervous messenger stammered, "the gentleman went away in a great hurry after the troops came. He had asked me to come and tell you if he could not get here himself tonight."

Jane felt herself flushing beneath the servant's questioning gaze. Her bitter disappointment at the broken rendezvous was overlaid by a sudden pang of fear. For young Simmons was a groom from her brother's stables, and she wondered how much he knew . . . or would tell.

"Oh . . . I see," she said, forcing her voice to remain calm, and wondering what motive the servant must be imagining had brought her to the lonely meadow at this ungodly hour. "Thank you, Simmons."

His unlined, honest features betraying no hint that he thought the situation odd or particularly scandalous, Simmons fumbled in the pocket of his greatcoat and produced a folded letter sealed with wax. "This is for you, miss," he stammered, bowing slightly and extending the letter to her.

"From him?" Abandoning all pretense of calm, Jane eagerly accepted the envelope and attempted to read the address in the dim light.

"No, miss. It's the letter *you* sent to him," Simmons replied. And in his voice Jane heard something that sounded like sympathy as he hurried to explain. "The gentleman had already gone before it could be gotten to him."

Simmons paused then, as if considering his next words carefully. "There was such a row up at the manor house," he finally continued. "Well, I thought you'd want to have your letter back . . ."

Jane tucked the letter into the folds of her cloak and looked up at him, realizing that in the groom she had found an ally who would not betray her indiscretion. "Thank you, Simmons," she said again. "That was very thoughtful of you."

She hesitated awkwardly, aware that such loyalty should be rewarded. "I am afraid I have no money with me at the moment—" she began. But before she could suggest that she would have something for him on the morrow Simmons cut her off with a wave of one big, work-hardened hand.

"Don't you worry, miss," the young groom assured her with dignity, "I didn't come here for money. The gentleman was very good to me while he was here." Then his broad features creased in a smile and in a gentler tone he asked, "Shall I see you home now, miss?"

"Thank you, no," Jane replied, the little catch in her voice promising that tears would very soon follow. "It is only a short walk. You have been very good."

Simmons bowed again, then, taking a step backward he put on his tall hat and climbed back onto the black horse. Once mounted he looked down at Jane and leaned closer so she could hear. "I never met no one like him," he said softly. "He's the *best* gentleman I ever knew."

Jane nodded in silent agreement, feeling the hot tears welling up in her eyes and wondering what magic her mysterious lover had wrought to engender such regard on the part of this simple country lad. For it had suddenly occurred to her that Simmons was also at risk, both for having slipped away from her brother's manor at this late hour, as well as for having allowed himself to become an instrument in her conspiracy.

She had no time for further reflection, for the black horse was stamping its hooves, impatient now to be back in its warm stable. "Do you think the gentleman will ever come back, miss?" Simmons's voice was a barely audible whisper above the snorting of the animal.

Jane slowly shook her head. "I fear he may not be able, Simmons," she replied. "You had better go now, before you are missed."

The servant straightened, touched the brim of his hat, then wheeled the horse around and rode away across the meadow. Jane watched him until he was once more swallowed up in the mist.

A bright tear ran down her cheek as she looked up at the lowering moon. "So this is how it is to end?" she asked the cloud-streaked sky.

Turning to the wood, she ran into the trees and back along the moonlit path the way she had come. Soon the dark outlines of a large stone house appeared through the trees. Warm light was shining from an upper window, and Jane knew that Cassandra had awakened and discovered her gone.

Making her way across the broad lawn at the rear of the house, Jane quietly let herself in through a low wooden door. Inside the kitchen the glow of embers in the fireplace provided the only light. Moving as quietly as possible across the flagged stone floor, Jane removed her cloak and hung it near the fireplace to dry. She took a candle in a copper holder from the mantel and lit it with a broom straw. Then, pausing just long enough to brush away her tears, she left the kitchen and walked through a dark hallway to the center of the house.

She had just reached the foot of the wide central staircase when she heard a footstep and saw the glimmering of another candle on the landing above.

"Jane, is that you?" Cassandra, her heavy plaits of golden hair falling about the shoulders of her nightgown, stood peering down into the dark stairwell, her soft features filled with concern.

"Yes, Cass, I am just coming up." Fixing a cheerful smile on her lips, Jane hurried upstairs. She reached the upper landing to find her older sister regarding her with frank amazement.

"Surely you have not been out again at this hour," Cassandra asked. "It is well past midnight."

"I felt like walking in the moonlight," Jane replied, brushing past the astonished Cass and making quickly for the door to her room.

"The moonlight?" Cassandra, who could always tell when Jane was lying, moved to block her way, forcing Jane to look directly into her steady gray eyes. "Jane, what have you been up to?"

Jane shrugged, attempting to inject a carefree note into her voice. "I have heard it said that Lord Byron highly commends the moonlight, when he is courting the muse," she replied brightly.

"And I have heard that the wicked young lord goes abroad at night only to court ladies of dubious reputation," Cassandra retorted. "What *have* you been doing, sister?"

Once again Jane felt her tears threatening to burst forth. She shook her head stubbornly. "I have done nothing either very dubious or very wicked," she replied. And in her mind's eye she glimpsed the handsome features of the man she had gone to meet. "I was not given an opportunity," she murmured with regret.

Cassandra's mouth fell open. But before she could find adequate words to express her shock, Jane kissed her on the cheek and pushed past her. "Good night, Cass," she whispered as she reached the door to her room.

Cassandra's lined features softened and she regarded her younger sister with concern. "Dearest Jane, you know you can confide in me," she said softly. "Please tell me what has happened?"

"Oh, Cass, I am not yet certain," Jane replied, feeling the salty wetness beginning to sting her cheeks. "Perhaps my foolish heart has been broken at last." She sniffled and managed a little smile. "I shall have to reflect on it and let you know in the morning."

Then without another word she entered her bedroom and firmly shut the door behind her, leaving Cassandra alone in the hallway to wonder.

Lit only by her single candle, the large, cheerful room that Jane loved so well by day was now a warren of leaping shadows. They danced impishly across the flowered wallpaper and pooled deep in the corners behind the bed as she walked to her mirrored vanity by the fireplace. Placing the candle on the table, Jane sat and began slowly taking down her elaborately curled hair, allowing the shining dark tresses to fall loose.

When she was done, she regarded her dim reflection in the mirror, raising one pale hand to touch the silvery-looking glass with her fingertips. "Only one of us is real," she said quietly to that other Jane who sat gazing at her from the glass, "the other is but an illusion. The question is, which am I?"

Removing the undelivered letter from her gown, she placed it on the dressing table before her and stared down at the address she had so neatly written there a lifetime ago. She was startled from her reverie by an insistent knocking at the door.

"Jane, do let me in," Cassandra entreated. "I will not sleep a wink until you have told me what has happened."

"What *has* happened?" Jane repeated in a voice so soft that only she could hear. "That, dear sister, is one thing that I will never tell you."

She scooped up the letter as Cassandra knocked again. "Jane!" she called, demanding now to be let in.

"Just a moment, Cass." With a heavy sigh Jane pushed back from the vanity, bowing to the inevitability of admitting her sister. Ever since they were small children Cass had always been the one who had soothed her hurts and given her the courage to go on. That would never change, certainly not now that *he* was gone.

Picking up the letter, she looked quickly around the dimly lit room. "And what *am* I to do with this?" she wondered aloud. For she could not reveal its contents, even to Cass, nor did she dare destroy it because of the secret it contained.

Jane caught her own worried reflection looking back at her from the shimmering depths of the mirror as Cass's knocking grew louder.

Volume One

Chapter 1

New York City
Present day

"**O**h, now I do like this!" Eliza Knight exclaimed, though there was no one within earshot.

She brushed a thick layer of dust from the mirror of the scarred little vanity table and peered into the silvery glass. The sudden appearance of her own reflection startled her and she paused for a moment to regard the hazy image. The familiar face looking back at her was, she thought, if not exactly beautiful, then slightly exotic, with its high cheekbones, straight if somewhat narrow nose and full lips. Her dark eyes were, she confirmed, still her best feature, though she also liked her glossy black hair, despite the longish, flyaway cut she'd let her hairdresser talk her into a couple of weeks before.

Grimacing at the hair, Eliza stepped back to take a better look at the old-fashioned rosewood dressing table. In the hour or so that she had been poking through the clutter of the shabby West Side antiques warehouse that was allegedly open only to the "Trade," the vanity was the only thing that had caught her eye. She had spied it just moments earlier, crammed between an art deco floor lamp and a Jetsons pink 1950s Formica coffee table, and had immediately felt herself drawn to it.

Taking her eyes from the dulled mirror, Eliza scanned the rows of dusty merchandise stretching in every direction like a bad Cubist painting. She finally spotted Jerry Shelburn three aisles away. He appeared to be taking stock of an ancient gasoline pump with a cracked glass top.

"Jerry," she called excitedly, "I want your opinion. Come over here and take a look at this!"

Jerry had gotten them admitted to the wholesaler's warehouse through one of his clients, who ran a small freight-forwarding business. Now he smiled good-naturedly and waved back. He carefully replaced the brass nozzle on the gas pump before starting toward her, the round lenses of his wire-framed glasses glittering like little moons beneath the cold fluorescents of the overhead fixtures.

Eliza sighed inwardly as she watched him picking his way through the maze of old furniture, noting the extraordinary care he took not to soil his Old Navy khakis and spotless cotton pullover. They had met two years earlier, through an artist friend of hers, when Eliza had been looking for someone to manage the small investment portfolio her father had left her. Jerry had turned out to be an excellent manager, increasing the value of her stocks by nearly thirty percent in the first year and then shrewdly using the capital to secure the down payment on the condo that also served as her studio, thus eliminating more than half the taxes she'd been paying as a renter.

Somehow while all of that was going on they had started dating and then, occasionally, sleeping together. It was marginally comfortable and definitely low maintenance on both sides. There had been a few times in recent months when she had felt as though the relationship was either going to progress into something more serious or end altogether, and had to admit that it wouldn't really bother her that much if it did end. Feeling slightly mercenary, she consoled herself with the thought that at least her net worth had never been higher.

Turning her attention back to the vanity table, Eliza dragged it out into the aisle and slowly ran her strong artist's hands over the marred top. Despite its numerous scratches, the old wood felt comfortably warm to her touch. The slightly formal, squared-off design vaguely reminded her of a Georgian piece she'd seen in one of her antique guidebooks, and she wondered how old it really was.

"So, what rare treasure have you uncovered?"

Eliza raised her eyes to the mirror and saw Jerry adjusting his glasses to peer over her shoulder.

"Look," she said, stepping away to afford him a clear view of the vanity, "isn't it adorable?"

"I thought you were looking for a floor lamp," he said, barely glancing at the table.

"I was," Eliza replied peevishly, "but I really like this. It's kind of charming, don't you think?"

"Hmmm . . ." Frowning as if he'd just been

served a piece of tainted fish, Jerry leaned over and examined a tiny pink sticker that Eliza hadn't noticed adhering to the side of the vanity. "At six hundred dollars it's not *that* charming," he sniffed. "Besides, the mirror's a mess." Jerry straightened and gave her a patronizing wink. "As your investment counselor, I heartily recommend going with a lamp."

Chapter 2

Fresh from a scalding shower, swaddled in her threadbare, old terry robe with her hair wrapped in a towel, Eliza stepped barefoot into her bedroom and regarded the prized vanity, which looked right at home among the mismatched collection of antique furniture filling the room.

"I really want your honest opinion now," she said, turning to look at the figure sprawled carelessly across the colorful patchwork quilt covering her Victorian-era four-poster bed. "Do you think I made an awful mistake?"

Wickham, an overweight gray tabby with a severe personality disorder, spread his considerable jaws wide and yawned to demonstrate his complete indifference to her question.

Not to be so easily deterred, Eliza scooped up the cat in her arms and crossed to the corner by the window, where Jerry had somewhat sullenly deposited the antique dressing table two hours earlier. The hazed rectangular mirror stood on the floor beside the table, leaning against the wall.

After admiring the newly acquired pieces for a moment Eliza sank cross-legged onto the carpet before them, cradling the squirming cat in her lap.

"I think the whole problem with Jerry and our relationship," she explained to Wickham, "can be summed up in this table. Because when I look at it I see something warm and beautiful. But all Jerry sees is a piece of used furniture. You're a creature of discerning taste. What do you see, Wickham?"

Eliza smiled and scratched the special spot between Wickham's ears. The cat's yellow eyes rolled back in his head and he stiffened and moaned in ecstasy.

"My point exactly!" Eliza gloated. "Because, unlike you and me, Jerry has no soul, just a bottom line." She released her grip on Wickham, who leaped out of her lap and settled himself comfortably on the carpet.

"It really is a lovely piece," she said, gently reaching to stroke the satiny finish of an unscarred table leg. It needed major cleaning and some linseed oil but she was pretty sure that it was very old.

As Eliza carefully removed the single drawer from the table, setting it on the floor before her, she noticed that it was lined with now-faded pink wallpaper that still retained a floral pattern. Ignoring the liner, she turned the drawer around and examined the outside corners, which had been fitted together without nails.

The slightly irregular dovetails holding the sides of the drawer together meant they were obviously cut by hand, reinforcing her belief that the table was old, crafted before the age of machine-made, mass-produced furniture.

Eliza smiled ruefully, for though she was entirely correct about the dovetails, she had also exhausted virtually the entire store of knowledge she remembered from the NYU evening extension class she'd taken two years earlier on appraising antique furniture.

Nevertheless, she turned the drawer over to inspect the bottom, vaguely recalling something about being sure the wood colors matched or didn't match or something. The pink liner fluttered to the floor, coming to rest upside down on the carpet.

Interested at last, Wickham swatted at the crumbling paper. Eliza shooed him away and then stared in surprise at the liner. For adhering to its underside was another strip of yellowing paper densely covered in cramped black type.

"Look, Wickham, it's a piece of . . . old newspaper!" she exclaimed, squinting to read the oddly shaped and embellished letters. "Listen to this," she breathed, tracing with her index finger a heavier line of print bannered across the top of the sheet: "THE HAMPSHIRE CHRONICLE, 7 APRIL, 1810 . . . My God, that was almost two hundred years ago!"

Her attention now riveted by the partial sheet of ancient newsprint, Eliza carefully lifted it onto the top of the vanity and spent the next few minutes curiously poring over several tightly packed columns of ads for "Gentlemen's best quality silk cravats," "beneficial beef extracts," "drayage and forwarding" (whatever they might be), and a host of other mysterious products with names like Gerlich's Female Potion, calibrated boiling thermometers and India rubber goods.

When finally her eyes tired of squinting at the strange, old-fashioned print she gave the sturdy little table another cursory inspection. Then she knelt beside the mirror and stood it upright, noticing again with some dismay that the silvered surface was, as Jerry had pointed out in the warehouse, badly worn.

Cheerfully dismissing the hazing as enhancing the overall charm of the piece, she experimentally tilted the mirror toward her and was distressed to see that the wood backing on one side was pulling away from the frame. "Oh, great! The backing seems to be warped," she murmured to the cat. "Now give me some support here, Wickham, I'd hate to have to admit that Jerry might have been right after all."

Wickham stretched and meowed.

"Thanks," Eliza grinned. "I needed that."

She pulled the mirror to her and turned it around to get a better look at the damaged backing. To her relief, though, the visible gap appeared to be no more than six inches long. "Well, it's not as bad as I thought," she said. "I think it only needs to be reglued." With her fingernail she experimentally lifted the edge of the backing from the mirror frame in an attempt to determine how far the separation extended. As she did so, something fell out of the mirror and landed on the carpet with a soft plop.

Attracted by the sudden motion, Wickham leaped onto the fallen object and hissed menacingly. Eliza pushed him away and stared at the thing in surprise. She slowly leaned the mirror back against the wall, then reached down and lifted the fallen object into the light.

She remained frozen on her knees for several seconds, gazing at her hand while she tried to reconstruct what had just happened. For she was holding a slim packet of thick, sepia-toned paper tied together like a Christmas package with a crisscross of bright green ribbon.

"Good Lord," she whispered, letting her eyes dart back to the mirror and glimpsing her own puzzled expression.

Something swatted against her hand and she looked down to see Wickham resolutely batting at the end of the bright ribbon. Snatching her hand away from him, she got to her feet and examined the packet more closely. Held together by the broad ribbon, she saw, were two rectangles of folded paper. The one on top was smaller than the other and had been written across in reddish brown ink, the words obscured by the ribbon covering them.

"Letters!" she exclaimed.

Eliza turned the packet over and saw that the larger of the two letters had been sealed with a blob of shiny red material that she guessed must be sealing wax, though it looked like no other wax she had ever seen, having more the consistency of brittle plastic. Intrigued, she carefully untied the ribbon securing the packet, so that she could read the address on the top envelope.

"'Miss Jane Austen, Chawton Cottage' . . . *Jane Austen!*"

Stunned by the name of the famous nineteenth-century author, Eliza paused and took a deep breath before she could read the remainder of the address on the letter. Jane Austen! Again she had to pause as her eyes raced ahead of her trembling lips. "'Jane Austen ~ Mr. Fitzwilliam Darcy, Chawton Great House,'" she squeaked.

Eliza stood there on her bedroom carpet for several more seconds, silently reading and rereading the words inscribed neatly across the front of the smaller envelope.

The thoughts racing through Eliza's head at that moment were somewhat difficult to define. For although she would not have classified herself as a voracious reader, she was well-enough read, her tastes running largely to popular fiction with a smattering of respectable old favorites, ranging from the works of Agatha Christie and Damon Runyon to a few major poets and several classical novelists.

And, like many women, one of Eliza's very favorite novels, numbered among half a dozen well-worn books occupying the small shelf beneath her bedside table, was *Pride and Prejudice*, Jane Austen's timeless story of Miss Elizabeth Bennet's uncompromising quest for a perfect love.

Which is only to say that Eliza Knight knew precisely who Jane Austen was, and she certainly knew who Fitzwilliam Darcy, the purported recipient of the letter she now held in her hand, was, or at least who he was supposed to be.

With the letters in her hand she went to the bed and sat down. Gazing at the window, her reflection surrounded by a moonlit halo, Eliza's imagination swirled with what ifs and could it bes. She smiled to herself. Jerry would be laughing and berating her for such romantic notions and, in truth, as wildly romantic as the idea was, it was ludicrous, patently absurd; because the relationship suggested by the enigmatic address on the letter was flatly impossible. Darcy was, after all, a fictitious character, wasn't he?

Looking down at Wickham, who had followed her to the bed, she said, "Well, there's only one way to find out: read the letters."

In spite of her well-founded skepticism as to the authenticity of the letters, Eliza felt her heart trip-hammer in her chest and her hands tremble as she opened the larger of the two letters: the one that was addressed to Jane Austen from Fitzwilliam Darcy with the broad, scrawled pen strokes of a man's hand. She read aloud:

12 May, 1810

Dearest Jane,
    The Captain has found me out. I am being forced to go into hiding immediately. But if I am able, I shall still be waiting at the same spot tonight. Then you will know everything you wish to know.

F. Darcy

Eliza paused to consider the meaning of those few sparse sentences. And when she began to read it over again there was a slight quaver in her voice. For this was not at all what she had expected. Though, on momentary reflection, she was not quite sure exactly what she had expected to find in Darcy's letter—some flowery romantic tribute, perhaps, or a poetic declaration of undying love to a lady fair. How odd . . . being found out, going into hiding. What did that mean? Maybe the other letter was Austen's reply and so held the answers.

Slipping the first letter behind the other in her hand, she examined it with awe. The lovely feminine handwriting flowed across the page and, turning it over in her hands, she saw that the sealing wax was still intact, a fanciful letter *A* impressed into it. This one had never been read, maybe never sent. Why? Tracing the curves of the seal with the tip of her finger she curiously experienced a tingling sensation that shot like a jolt of electricity through her body.

"Wickham, can you imagine what it would mean if the letter really was written by Jane Austen?" She looked at the cat, who was unconcernedly applying his long pink tongue to one of his wickedly clawed front paws. Eliza sighed, "No, of course you can't, you poor thing, you have no forehead."

Looking at the letter she turned it over and over again in her hands. If it was genuine and she opened it, she would forever be known as the stupid artist who ruined a historic document.

Before she burned her bridges, Eliza decided she needed to try and find out something about the fictitious Mr. Darcy. Maybe the Internet would give her the answers she sought.

Chapter 3

In sharp contrast to Eliza's bedroom—which, with its eclectic collection of old wooden furniture, framed prints and warm fabric accents, could only be described as cozy—the living room of her small condo (actually the workroom and studio where she created her art and operated her Internet gallery) was all twenty-first-century business.

In front of the large window that allowed her to look directly into the wheelhouses of passing freighters on the East River were arrayed her white IKEA computer desk and drawing board, and beside them the wide steel filing cabinets, airbrush, paints and other equipment necessary to her work.

Hanging on the otherwise bare walls were several meticulous illustrations of the idyllic, flower-filled country landscapes and other natural and whimsical subjects in which she specialized.

With the envelopes in her hand and her bare feet tucked into a pair of warm sheepskin moccasins, Eliza crossed the polished hardwood floor of her studio and seated herself on the tall chrome-and-leather stool at her drawing board. Taking care first to cover the painting of a woodland cottage to which she'd been adding a mistily airbrushed backdrop of thickly forested mountains, she laid the two envelopes on the board side by side and switched on her halogen work light.

Outside the moon caressed the surface of the river with a ribbon of silver light and while her rational mind believed firmly that the letters were some kind of elaborate hoax, she couldn't stop the flights of fancy inspired by the implausible correspondence. Shaking off the romantic thoughts as silly schoolgirl fantasies, Eliza shooed Wickham out of the desk chair and sat down in front of her computer console. Signing onto the Internet, she called up a popular search engine and typed in "Jane Austen."

The computer whirred softly for several seconds before the screen was filled with the information she requested. Eliza stared at her monitor in disbelief; there were over a million and a half Web sites. Looking over at the cat now perched on the high stool, she sighed, "I thought this was going to be easy." Looking back at the monitor she found an array of Web sites pertaining to the author. Scrolling down through the list, Eliza discovered to her amazement that there were sites devoted to Jane Austen's life, her birthplace, the times in which she lived, each of her books and all the movies and television shows that had ever been made from the books. There were even more Web sites devoted to the actors in the movies and television shows made from the books. In addition to those, there were hundreds of fan sites, history sites, sites for scholarly discussions of Jane Austen's work, and sites devoted to the many sequels to Jane Austen books, written in the style of the author by latter-day imitators.

There were Japanese Jane Austen Web sites, Australian Web sites, Norwegian sites, discussion sites about Jane Austen's letters, her family, her friends . . . the list went on and on.

Eliza scrolled until her finger ached and her eyes grew bleary, and yet she realized that she hadn't even made a dent in the endless list. "Where do I start?" she groaned to Wickham.

After several more minutes of scrolling she sat back, rubbed her eyes and blinked at the screen again. The title and description of one Web site in particular suddenly caught her eye.

"Austenticity.com," she read, liking the sound of it. "'Everything you ever wanted to know about Jane Austen.' Now that sounds promising," she told the cat.

Wickham rubbed against Eliza's arm as she clicked onto the site. A burst of romantic theme music suddenly poured from the computer's speakers and a title popped up onto the screen:

AUSTENTICITY.COM PRESENTS
Jane Austen's
PRIDE AND PREJUDICE

The title faded away as a scene from the BBC/ A&E television miniseries *Pride and Prejudice* began to play on the computer screen. In the scene,

Elizabeth Bennet and Mr. Darcy were alone in a sitting room.

Eliza found her lips moving in silent accompaniment to the actor playing Darcy as he recited one of her favorite lines from P&P: "You must allow me to tell you how ardently I admire and love you . . ."

Her face reddening, Eliza abruptly broke off the monologue and turned down the sound, smiling at the casual ease with which she had been captivated.

"Darcy, you seductive devil!" She grinned at the now-silent actor still mouthing his lines. "I dearly love your first proposal to Elizabeth Bennet," she told him. "But right now I need some hard information about the real *you!* If there *was* a real you."

She stopped the film clip by clicking onto the information menu at the top of her computer screen. Another screen immediately popped up, featuring a rather dour portrait of the author herself beneath a new title:

AUSTENTICITY.COM
The Everything Austen Site

CAN'T GET ENOUGH JANE AUSTEN?
Dying to know what she ate and wore, what books she read, songs she sang? Post your question on our message boards.
One of our Austen experts is sure to have the answer you seek.

"Austen experts! Now that's more like it," Eliza said, reading the message. She examined the several topics on the message boards, selected one titled "Jane's Life & Times" and started to type.

POST MESSAGE:

Was Darcy from *Pride and Prejudice* a *real* person?
Please reply by e-mail to: SMARTIST@galleri. com

Smiling to herself, she sent the message.

"There!" she told Wickham. "With any luck, somebody will have the solution to our little mystery right at their fingertips."

The cat rolled his yellow eyes up at her, as if to say, Don't kid yourself.

Eliza shrugged and closed out the Austenticity Web site. "Okay," she grudgingly conceded, peering once more at the daunting list of other Internet sites. "I'll look at a few more, but I'm not going to keep doing this all night."

❧

More than an hour later a thoroughly exhausted Eliza sat propped among the pillows piled against the elaborately carved figurals decorating the headboard of her bed.

As she leafed idly through her copy of *Pride and Prejudice* her imagination was filled with the possibilities presented by the two mysterious letters. Out of the corner of her eye she could see the little vanity table by the window, she wondered who had placed the letters behind the mirror, and for what possible purpose.

Wickham was comfortably dozing on the pillows beside her as she finally put her book aside and switched off the bedside lamp. Moonlight filled the room, casting soft reflections in the hazed mirror of the vanity table. Eliza gazed sleepily at the golden orb outside her window and snuggled down next to the cat.

"You must allow me to tell you how ardently I admire and love you . . ." she murmured dreamily. "Oh God, Wickham, that is *so* romantic! Could there have been a flesh-and-blood Darcy who actually spoke those words to Jane Austen *before* she wrote them?"

Wickham's deep-throated purr rumbled up from somewhere inside, indicating that he was already fast asleep.

Eliza's exploration of the Internet had provided her with no more clues to the existence of a real-life Fitzwilliam Darcy than the letters had. However, she had discovered that most scholars believed Jane Austen peopled her novels with characters from her own life. Sighing deeply she wondered about the man who had inspired one of the most romantic characters ever written.

If Darcy had been a real person, she wondered, were they in love, how did they meet, why didn't they marry? Reminding herself that Darcy's note was not a love letter, she questioned the identity of the captain and what he had found out about Darcy. Eliza sleepily entwined her fingers in the warm ruff of fur around Wickham's neck.

She tried to imagine herself in the arms of a passionate, ardent lover. The fantasy was interrupted by an extremely unsatisfying image of